Samuel French Acting Edition

I0591831

How Green Was My Brownie

A Comedy in Three Acts

by Jack Sharkey

SAMUELFRENCH.COM   SAMUELFRENCH.CO.UK

FOR PRODUCTION ENQUIRIES

UNITED STATES AND CANADA
Info@SamuelFrench.com
1-866-598-8449

UNITED KINGDOM AND EUROPE
Plays@SamuelFrench.co.uk
020-7255-4302

Each title is subject to availability from Samuel French, depending upon country of performance. Please be aware that *HOW GREEN WAS MY BROWNIE* may not be licensed by Samuel French in your territory. Professional and amateur producers should contact the nearest Samuel French office or licensing partner to verify availability.

Please refer to page 104 for further copyright information.

SYNOPSIS

Who is going crazy in the Flinder household? Is it WINIFRED FLINDER, supposedly just out of the hospital, who insists she actually spent the two weeks living it up in Paris? Is it ADDISON FLINDER, her husband, who thinks his wife plans to go into the convent? Is it their daughter BONNIE, who suspects both her parents are a bit nuts? Or is it nurse MAXINE THREADGILL, who thinks the neighboring piano teacher is a great pediatric surgeon— or gynecologist PHILIP MORGAN, who gratefully accepts payment for an operation he may not have performed— or GUNTHER CHOWDY, the general handyman who insists the brownies have it in for the Flinders—or housekeeper NORA LARKIN, who expects at any moment to be murdered in her bed? Perhaps it's LORELEI GULLOCK, a neighbor whose purse contains anything from crowbars to teddy bears, or her nephew TONY METZEL, who thinks he can psychoanalyze a person in a roomful of people with no one being the wiser, or HENRI MARNIER, a Frenchman who hopes to parlay garlic, oregano and Roquefort into the latest rage in men's toiletries. Maybe it's even WALDO LENNIMER, a Doctor of Musicology who blames his ill fortune on neglecting to leave the brownies a saucer of milk. Whoever it is, when you plunk a group like this down into the heart of Tarrytown, New York, you can expect a lot of confusion, an unsolicited appearance of The Headless Horseman, and a lot of terrified screams from the characters, not to mention hilarious shrieks from the audience in this are-there-or-aren't-there jaunt through the superstition-ridden environs of Washington Irving country, where anything can happen—and eventually does.

CAST OF CHARACTERS

ADDISON FLINDER, *president of* Titan, Inc. *Products for Men*

WINIFRED FLINDER, *his wife*

BONNIE FLINDER, *their daughter and* ADDISON'S *secretary*

NORA LARKIN, *the* FLINDERS' *housekeeper*

LORELEI GULLOCK, *a friend of* WINIFRED

MAXINE THREADGILL, *a registered nurse*

PHILIP MORGAN, *a gynecologist*

GUNTHER CHOWDY, *a general handyman*

WALDO LENNIMER, *a piano teacher*

TONY METZEL, *Lorelei's nephew*

HENRI MARNIER, *a marketing research assistant*

TIME: The Present

LOCALE: The Flinder Home near Tarrytown, N.Y.

ACT ONE
A pleasant midafternoon in August

ACT TWO
That evening

ACT THREE
The following morning

How Green
Was My Brownie

ACT ONE

Curtain rises on the FLINDER *home near Tarrytown, New York. Decor is modern/rustic, giving the impression of having been built by a very wealthy pioneer. The scene is a single room, a sort of living-room/recreation-room combination. Wide double doors directly Upstage Center reveal a modest patio backed by a low stone wall, beyond which we can see a sylvan backdrop suggesting a piney woods. Directly Left of these doors, but angled to face toward Downstage Right, is a somewhat mammoth fireplace. Beginning just below and a bit Left of this fireplace is the foot of an unrailed staircase, which curves up around the fireplace and out of sight in just a few steps. A short thrust of wall flanking part of the Downstage side of the staircase forms an angle with the room wall, into which is tucked a businesslike desk with a chair and telephone. Upon the wall overlooking desk and chair from behind is a stuffed moosehead. Just below this part of the Left wall is the entry to a foyer leading to the front door of the house. A highbacked chair is set against the wall below the foyer entry. Directly opposite this entry in the Downstage Right wall is the double-action swingdoor leading to the kitchen. Between this door and the patio doors, an L-shaped bar with matching stools is tucked into the Upstage Right angle of the Right wall, with a tidy supply of bottled liquor on a shelf behind the bar. Just Right of Downstage Center is a low round cocktail table, semicircled above by two abutted segments of a sectional sofa. It is midafternoon in August, and*

*the entire room is bright and sunny. At curtain-rise,
the stage is empty. A moment later,* BONNIE FLINDER
*appears on the patio. She is 23 years old, very pretty,
and carries a large armload of gladiolas. She steps
just inside the room, looks about, and then:*

BONNIE. (*Calls out cheerily.*) Hello? Anybody here?
(*Goes to bar, sets flowers on it, dusts hands.*) Nora,
where are you?

NORA. (*Off, Left.*) Is that you, Miss Bonnie? (*Appears
on stairs, bustling down, a large and not oppressively
motherly woman.*) Oh, good morning, dear. I was just
airing out the bedrooms. They still smell of wet plaster
and varnish. (NORA *crosses to* BONNIE *on:*)

BONNIE. Mother isn't here yet? I brought her some
flowers. Do we have anything to put them in?

NORA. I think so. The dishes aren't all unpacked, but
I (*Starts for kitchen.*) seem to remember that big green
bowl thing— (*Exits into kitchen.*)

BONNIE. (*Surveys fireplace.*) Say, that's some fireplace.
Is it just for show, or does it work?

NORA. (*Off.*) I'm sure it's the real McCoy. You know
your father!

BONNIE. (*Nods as she examines fireplace.*) Nothing but
the best for Addison Flinder. (NORA *enters with shallow
green bowl during:*) Do you know, last summer in Paris,
Dad drove the waiters crazy insisting on *imported* champagne!

NORA. (*Has looked for site, decided on table, and left
bowl there, heading toward flowers on bar.*) These are
lovely. I've always been partial to gladiolas. The smell
makes me think of funeral homes. I do enjoy a nice wake.
(*Takes flowers, starts for bowl, where she will subse-
quently arrange them in a low-lying pattern.*)

BONNIE. They are nice, aren't they! I saw them as I
drove up, and couldn't resist picking them. I thought
they'd lift Mother's spirits.

NORA. I'm sure they will. Your mother enjoys a good wake, herself.

BONNIE. (*About to protest this recurring image.*) Nora, I wish you wouldn't—

NORA. (*Straightens up from arranging flowers.*) Did you say you saw them driving in? Where in the world did you see flowers nice as these? I thought they were store-bought.

BONNIE. Why—right in our garden, Nora. At the bottom of the drive? Our new handyman must really be handy.

NORA. If you mean he's got a green thumb, from these I'd say so. If you mean available, you're wrong. He's two hours late, half the things are still unpacked, and your mother's due any minute.

BONNIE. (*Gets first sight of moosehead, reacts.*) Whose idea was *that?!*

NORA. Your father thought it would give the room a nice outdoorsy touch.

BONNIE. But it's hovering right over my desk. I don't know if I can work with that thing staring down my neck!

NORA. (*Starts for kitchen.*) Count your blessings. He came *that* close to getting a totem pole. (*Exits.*)

BONNIE. (*Grateful, but curious.*) What stopped him?

NORA. (*Off.*) One of its carved heads reminded him of your grandmother.

BONNIE. Mother's mother or his?

NORA. What do *you* think? The *moose* looks like *his!* (BONNIE *laughs at this just as the PHONE rings.*)

BONNIE. I'll get it, Nora! (*Picks up phone.*) *Titan, Incorporated!* Good morning! . . . Oh, hello, Mrs. Gullock . . . It is? . . . (*Looks at wristwatch.*) Okay, then —good afternoon! . . . Yes, we're running the business from here for awhile. It was Dad's idea—he wants to stay close to Mother till she's convalesced a bit . . . (*Listens, looks dismayed at what she is hearing, but keeps most of the dismay out of her voice, on:*) Today? Oh, gee, I don't know—I mean, it's her first day home from the hospital, and— (*Listens, screwing up face unhappily at what she hears, then defeatedly admits:*) Well—no—the doctor didn't *absolutely* say she shouldn't have visitors, Mrs. Gullock, but—well—we're not quite unpacked, or anything, and it's rather a mess . . . (NORA *enters from kitchen with small pitcher of water, waters flowers in bowl, but turns head slightly to listen to* BONNIE, *during:*) Well, yes, I'm sure we could use a hand, but I hate to put you to such trouble . . . All right. Yes. In about fifteen minutes. We'll be looking for you. Yes. 'Bye now. (*Hangs up wearily.*) That was Mrs. Gullock.

NORA. (*Horrified.*) That woman's not coming over here today?

BONNIE. I intimated it was a bad time . . . almost implied she wasn't welcome.

NORA. That means she's coming. She'd never pass up a challenge like that. (*Heads for stairs.*) I think I'll unpack the aspirin. (*Hands pitcher to* BONNIE *as she passes and starts up stairs.*)

BONNIE. I suppose it's too late to put up a "No Trespassing" sign—?

NORA. (*Ascending.*) What makes you think she can read? (*She is gone.*)

(BONNIE *is facing up staircase, and so does not see* GUNTHER CHOWDY *appear at patio doors; he is middle-aged, not unhandsome in a burly fashion, and carries a soft workman's cap in one hand and a large horseshoe in the other; he sees* BONNIE, *comes in and arrives directly behind her, during:*)

BONNIE. (*Calling after* NORA.) Too bad the new handyman's not here. We could have him dig a moat! (*Half to* NORA, *half to herself, turning:*) Of course, if it worked, we'd also have to do without *Mother*—! (*Sees* GUNTHER, *reacts.*) Oh! Who—?

GUNTHER. I'm sorry if I scared you. I was looking for Mrs. Larkin.

BONNIE. Nora's just gone upstairs . . . Would you be our new handyman?

GUNTHER. That all depends . . .

BONNIE. On what?

GUNTHER. Were you serious about that moat?

BONNIE. *That* depends— Can you *dig* one? No, forget it. It's just one of those days. (*Extends her hand.*) I'm Bonnie Flinder— (GUNTHER *succeeds in transferring cap to hand holding horseshoe, takes her hand, on:*) *Are* you Mister Chowdy?

GUNTHER. At your service—excluding moats. By the way, I'm sorry to be so late, but I had trouble finding a horseshoe.

BONNIE. Why don't you carry a rabbit's foot like everyone else? (*Realizes they are still joined.*) Uh—if you don't mind—

GUNTHER. (*Swiftly releases her hand.*) Oh, sorry. I thought I was still holding the horseshoe.

BONNIE. Flattery will get you nowhere. What's the horseshoe *for,* anyhow?

GUNTHER. You father wants one nailed over your front door, for luck.

BONNIE. You're kidding. No, wait—Dad *did* say Tarrytown was a superstitious spot. This could be his way of keeping up with the local Joneses.

GUNTHER. I hope *he* wasn't kidding. I had to drive clear to Valhalla to find one. That's a town just east of here.

BONNIE. Well, I didn't think you'd swiped it from a Valkyrie.

GUNTHER. You must be from New York City.

BONNIE. Because I don't know the territory?

GUNTHER. No, because you make wisecracks instead of conversation. (BONNIE *gapes, but he continues as if his last remark had been innocuous:*) Well, I guess I better get this thing nailed up before your father gets here— (*Stops as* NORA *appears on stairs carrying small aspirin bottle.*) Oh, hi there, Mrs. Larkin!

NORA. (*Descends into room on:*) Well! If it isn't the *late* Gunther Chowdy! About time you got here. (*Takes pitcher from* BONNIE, *who is still somewhat stunned, starts for kitchen, then turns, puzzled.*) Is there anything wrong, Miss Bonnie?

BONNIE. (*Recovering slightly.*) N-no. Mister Chowdy was— It's not his fault he's late. He was on a secret mission for Dad. Buying a horseshoe. (GUNTHER *holds it up.*)

NORA. I'm not going to ask what for.

GUNTHER. All right.

NORA. (*Walks as far as kitchen door, stops, then turns in resignation to face him.*) All right—what for?

BONNIE. To bring this house nothing but good luck.

NORA. Good. If it works, we won't need these aspirin. (*Exits to kitchen.*)

GUNTHER. Inside joke?

BONNIE. My, a direct question! Aren't you afraid I'll answer with a wisecrack?

GUNTHER. I'll take my chances.

BONNIE. You took a pretty big one a moment ago.

GUNTHER. You mean my chances of working for you? I work for your father.

BONNIE. Mister Chowdy, one ride to Valhalla does not a workday make! Now suppose you just go hammer up that horseshoe, and maybe I *won't* speak to Dad about you!

GUNTHER. If you're trying to strike terror into my heart, perhaps I ought to tell you the facts of Tarrytown life, Miss Flinder. You see—

NORA. (*Pokes head in from kitchen.*) Would anybody like a sandwich?

GUNTHER. With mayonnaise.

NORA. And what?

GUNTHER. Bread would be nice.

NORA. Miss Bonnie?

BONNIE. I'm too busy. Which is more than I can say for Mister Chowdy!

NORA. I'll see that your father has a talk with him—if *you* ever finish. (*Pops back into kitchen.*)

BONNIE. (*After an uncomfortable pause.*) Nora's from New York City, too. (GUNTHER *laughs.*) I guess maybe I *was* being a little flippant with you. I'm sorry. As for that inside joke about the aspirin— Do you know a Lorelei Gullock?

GUNTHER. Almost everyone around here knows Mrs. Gullock.

BONNIE. Well, she's stopping by in a few minutes. Does that explain the aspirin?

GUNTHER. Arsenic is quicker.

BONNIE. We weren't going to give it to *her*. Of course, we could always exceed the recommended dosage.

GUNTHER. Minutes later—your headache's gone! But how do you ditch the body?

BONNIE. (*Laughs.*) You seem to know her quite well.

GUNTHER. I work for her.

BONNIE. I thought you worked for *us*—?

GUNTHER. Well, see, I'm not exclusive. You might call me a kind of general factotum for Tarrytown.

BONNIE. Oh— *That's* the "facts of life" you were going to tell me!

GUNTHER. Carpentry here, a leaky pipe there, a little gardening now and then—

BONNIE. Oh, speaking of gardening— (*Moves down toward bowl.*) —I hope you don't mind—this morning on the way in—they were so lovely—I picked these.

GUNTHER. No—*I* don't mind if Doctor Lennimer doesn't.

BONNIE. I don't understand— Who is Doctor Lennimer?

GUNTHER. The big white colonial on the hill down by the main road—?

BONNIE. The neighboring house? Oh—Gunther— Mister Chowdy—

GUNTHER. Gunther.

BONNIE. Mister Chowdy—are you trying to tell me—

Oh, please say that Doctor Lennimer doesn't have a garden beside our driveway!

GUNTHER. Not *now*, he doesn't!

BONNIE. Oh, dear! (*Remembers:*) You know—there was a man at the upstairs window of that house when I was picking these. He was waving at me. I thought he was just being friendly. I waved back and kept right on picking.

GUNTHER. What did he do?

BONNIE. I don't know. When I looked again, he wasn't in the window.

GUNTHER. Probably fainted. You're lucky he didn't take a shot at you.

BONNIE. There must be some way I can explain to him.

GUNTHER. There is. They call it "Long Distance."

BONNIE. It would have been so nice for Mother—having a doctor right next door. A friendly doctor, I mean. (NORA *enters with a sandwich on a small plate, joins them, during:*)

GUNTHER. Your Mother's an invalid?

BONNIE. No. Convalescing. She just had a hysterectomy.

NORA. (*Scandalized.*) Miss Bonnie! When I was your age, ladies didn't *talk* about things like that!

BONNIE. Nora, when you were my age, ladies didn't *know* about things like that! They just went all hysterical and grew moustaches!

NORA. (*Stiffly.*) But not in that order! (*Hands plate to* GUNTHER, *starts back toward kitchen.*)

BONNIE. Nora's just a little uptight. Mother never had a hysterectomy before . . . Boy, *that* was dumb!

NORA. (*Without turning.*) We're *all* a little uptight, today, is *my* guess! (*Exits to kitchen.*)

BONNIE. But, about Doctor Lennimer—do you think if I apologized, he might consider—oh—just being around if Mother needs him?

GUNTHER. If her fingers aren't too stiff.

BONNIE. Her fingers?

GUNTHER. Miss Flinder—your neighbor is a Doctor of Musicology. He teaches piano lessons.

BONNIE. Oh! But he calls himself "Doctor" Lennimer?

GUNTHER. Well, "Fingers" Lennimer sounds kind of crooked. (NORA *rushes out of kitchen.*)

NORA. They're here! I just saw the car coming round the turn!

GUNTHER. (*Hands plate to* BONNIE.) I'd better get that horseshoe up! (*Starts for patio.*)

NORA. You haven't touched your sandwich.

GUNTHER. Too much mayonnaise.

BONNIE. (*Hands plate to* NORA.) And he talks about New Yorkers! (*DOOR CHIMES sound.*) Oh, there they are!

NORA. (*Hands plate to* GUNTHER.) Here! I've got to get the door.

GUNTHER. (*Starts out patio doors.*) So I'll nail it up after lunch. (*He is gone.* NORA *is heading for foyer as DOOR CHIMES sound again.*)

NORA. Coming! I'm coming! (*Exits to front door.*)

ADDISON. (*Off.*) Hello, Nora! Would you give Nurse Threadgill a hand with Winifred? (ADDISON *enters, carrying small overnight bag; he is big, rubicund, and has a rather booming deep voice; he continues speaking to unseen* NORA:) I'll bring her things up to her room. (*Starts for stairs, notices* BONNIE, *speaks without pausing:*) Hello, dear. How's business? (BONNIE *opens her mouth, but he is already vanishing up the stairs, so she shrugs, and:*)

BONNIE. (*To no one in particular.*) Booming.

NORA. (*Off.*) Easy now, dear. Just you keep a good hold on my arm . . .

(NORA *enters supporting the right arm of* WINIFRED FLINDER, *a slender grayhaired lady of about 55 in a crisp lightweight cotton skirt and jacket and somewhat frilly blouse, with a small flowered hat perched on her head;* WINIFRED *is patiently submitting to being assisted, for courtesy's sake, but doesn't really need help. Supporting her other arm comes* MAXINE THREADGILL, *a registered nurse in sensible shoes—white, of course—white nurse's stockings, dress and starched cap, and a short lightweight blue cape;* MAXINE'S *face and demeanor reflect dedication and pride in her hallowed profession, as though anything she does—even eating a hamburger—is somehow intrinsically selfless and noble. The attitudes of* NORA *and* MAXINE *are those of people who have just rescued someone from a foundering ocean liner; the attitude of* WINIFRED—*only slightly concealed—is that of someone who would rather have gone down with the ship than endure all the fuss of rescue. Halfway across the room toward the sofas,* WINIFRED *halts;* NORA *and* MAXINE *halt with her.*)

WINIFRED. What is this place? Where have you brought me?

NORA. Why, this is your home, dear.

WINIFRED. Then why don't I recognize it?

BONNIE. (*Comes forward, speaks with gruff warmth.*) Now-now, Mother, you're being forgetful again. I *told* you about the new house. This is where we'll be living from now on. Doctor Morgan said the country would be good for you.

WINIFRED. Oh, yes. I *had* forgotten. (*Permits* NORA *and* MAXINE *to take her toward sofas, again, on:*) I'm sorry, Bonnie.

MAXINE. Here, Mrs. Flinder—why don't you sit down and get used to it? (*Helps* WINIFRED *sit down, as:*)

NORA. (*Starts for stairs.*) I'll have your room ready in a minute. (*Exits up the stairs, during:*)

WINIFRED. I don't think I can get used to it in a minute.

MAXINE. Well, now, you don't have to go up to your room if you don't want to.

BONNIE. Would you like a nice cup of tea? It'll only take a minute.

WINIFRED. Everything only takes a minute—why is that?

MAXINE. Life has a way of rushing by . . . (*Gets look from* BONNIE, *goes on hurriedly to* WINIFRED:) . . . present company excepted.

BONNIE. I'll just see about that tea. (*Starts for kitchen.*)

WINIFRED. I'm not sure I want any tea. (BONNIE *hesitates.*)

MAXINE. Nonsense, Mrs. Flinder. It'll do you good. (BONNIE *starts for kitchen again.*)

WINIFRED. I'd rather have a highball. (BONNIE *stops, and* ADDISON *comes downstairs into room on:*)

BONNIE. Oh, Mother—do you think you should?

WINIFRED. Nobody has a highball because they should. I just want one.

ADDISON. (*Crosses solicitously to side of sofa.*) Remember, Winifred, you just got out of the hospital.

WINIFRED. All the more reason. Two weeks on the wagon is murder.

BONNIE. What do you think, Nurse?

MAXINE. Well—Doctor Morgan didn't *forbid* drinking, but—

WINIFRED. I don't like Doctor Morgan. He smiles too much. And he rubs his hands.

ADDISON. That's just his bedside manner. A doctor has to be friendly.

WINIFRED. Not that friendly. (*To* BONNIE:) He looks under ladies' dresses!

MAXINE. He's a gynecologist. His interest in women is purely pathological.

BONNIE. Would you care to rephrase that?

ADDISON. Bonnie—!

BONNIE. I'll just go see about that tea.

WINIFRED. I don't want tea. I want a highball. (NORA *enters from stairs on:*)

ADDISON. Now-now!

NORA. Now-now what?

WINIFRED. Now-now I want a *highball*, now-now!

NORA. Oh, of course, dear. I'll get it for you. (*Starts toward bar.*)

ADDISON. Uh—Nora—we're not sure it's wise, not sure at all.

NORA. Well, while you're making up your minds, I'll make the highball.

BONNIE. While you're at it, Nora, I'll have a small brandy.

ADDISON. Isn't it a bit early in the day?

BONNIE. Lorelei Gullock is coming over.

ADDISON. Who told her our new address?!

WINIFRED. She probably got it from Doctor Morgan.

BONNIE. So much for privileged communications!

ADDISON. I wish you wouldn't talk that way about Doctor Morgan, dear.

WINIFRED. Bonnie doesn't like him, either, Addison.

ADDISON. Well, she should! He's—uh—still *single*, you know.

MAXINE. (*Dreamily.*) I know! (*When* OTHERS *all look at her:*) Why shouldn't I know? It's a fact. He's never been married.

NORA. (*Coming from bar with a highball and a small brandy.*) So much for his bedside manner! (ADDISON *is about to speak, but stops as a loud HAMMERING is heard off Left.*)

MAXINE. What's that?

BONNIE. (*Taking brandy from* NORA.) The new handyman is nailing a horseshoe over our front door.

WINIFRED. (*Taking highball from* NORA.) What in the world for?

ADDISON. It's supposed to bring good luck to the house. (*The DOOR CHIMES sound.*)

NORA. That must be Mrs. Gullock.

BONNIE. So much for horseshoes! (*Drains her brandy glass.*)

WINIFRED. (*Stands.*) I think I'll drink this in my room. Bonnie, would you show me the way?

BONNIE. (*Hands empty glass to* NORA, *takes* WINI-FRED'S *arm, on:*) I'm new here, too, Mother. Let's go find it together. (*They head for stairs. DOOR CHIMES sound again.*)

ADDISON. Isn't anybody going to answer the door?

NORA. (*Holds empty glass up as she heads for kitchen.*) I've got to do the dish. (*Exits.*)

ADDISON. Bonnie—?

BONNIE. I'm helping Mother find her room.

LORELEI. (*Off Left.*) Yoo-hoo! It's Lorelei! Winifred, are you here? (*Enters from foyer; she is a large sturdy woman, toting a shoulderstrap purse, probably containing anything from spare shoes to turtle food.*) The door was unlocked, so I just barged in!

WINIFRED. (*Reverses direction so she is apparently just coming downstairs.*) Lorelei, darling! How nice!

LORELEI. (*Takes* WINIFRED'S *hands.*) Winifred Flinder! You look absolutely ghastly! (*Leads her toward sofa.*) It must have been terrible, absolutely terrible. You just sit down here, now, and tell me all about it!

MAXINE. You mustn't excite yourself, Mrs. Flinder.

LORELEI. (*Sitting beside* WINIFRED *on sofa, looks up at* MAXINE, *takes in garb.*) Is this your nurse?

BONNIE. How did you guess?

ADDISON. Bonnie—! (*DOOR CHIMES sound.*)

MAXINE. (*With ill-concealed excitement.*) That must be Doctor Morgan!

BONNIE. (*Starts for kitchen.*) I think I'll give Nora a hand with the dish.

ADDISON. You'll stay right where you are, young lady!

WINIFRED. (*Starts to rise.*) Then *I'll* give Nora a hand with the dish!

ADDISON. Winifred Flinder, you'll do no such thing! (*DOOR CHIMES sound again.*)

LORELEI. (*Rising.*) Tell you what—*I'll* let Doctor Morgan in!

ADDISON. Oh, *would* you, Lorelei?

BONNIE. Try and stop her. (*Exits to kitchen.*)

LORELEI. What did Bonnie mean by that?

ADDISON. Uh— When there's a good deed to be done, nothing stops Lorelei Gullock!

LORELEI. Why, how nice! (*Exits through foyer.*)

WINIFRED. Addison, that's *not* what Bonnie meant!

ADDISON. I won't have our daughter insulting our friends.

WINIFRED. What's that got to do with Lorelei?

(LORELEI *enters with* DOCTOR PHILIP MORGAN; *he is medium tall, nattily dressed, and wears an unctuous smile as he stops just inside room and rubs his hands; just an instant before his appearance,* MAXINE *has grabbed up* WINIFRED'S *wrist, and stares down studiously at her wristwatch, forming "an image of brisk efficiency" for* PHILIP *to notice; she can't resist peeking up at him to see if it's coming off; it isn't;* PHILIP *is looking only at* WINIFRED. MAXINE *reluctantly stops her pose as he speaks:*)

PHILIP. Well, well, well! And how is our little patient feeling today?

WINIFRED. Better. (*Takes swallow of highball; then:*) And better.

LORELEI. She's being very brave, Philip. I haven't heard her complain even once!

PHILIP. What's that you're drinking, Winifred?

WINIFRED. A scotch highball.

MAXINE. I told her you wouldn't approve, Doctor.

PHILIP. Why did you tell her that, Miss Threadgill?

ADDISON. You mean you *do* approve? I thought in her condition—

PHILIP. Best thing in the world for her. Matter of fact, I'd like one myself!

MAXINE. (*Eagerly.*) Let *me* fix it for you, Doctor!

ADDISON. Nonsense. What do we have servants for? I'll tell Nora—

LORELEI. No, let me—!

ADDISON. (*Sees* LORELEI *is already en route to kitchen, so:*) Well, if you wouldn't mind, Lorelei . . .

WINIFRED. (*As* LORELEI *exits.*) Of course she wouldn't mind. She's dying to see my kitchen. As a matter of fact —so am I! (*Rises, starts toward kitchen.*)

MAXINE. Do you need any help?

WINIFRED. To keep my eyes open? I don't think so . . . (*Exits to kitchen.*)

ADDISON. Philip—level with me—do you really think Winifred should be drinking?

PHILIP. (*Solemnly.*) Addison—you ought to know something about your wife.

ADDISON. After twenty-five years, I should hope so!

PHILIP. I mean about her condition.

MAXINE. (*Helpfully.*) He means about her condition.

ADDISON. You told me she was going to be fine.

PHILIP. And she is. Physically.

MAXINE. Yes, physically.

PHILIP. Miss Threadgill, if I want your help—

MAXINE. Just ask! Anything! Whatever you say, Doctor!

PHILIP. Then please stop *echoing* whatever I say!

MAXINE. Echoing?

ADDISON. Philip—! What *about* Winifred? You don't mean she's—?

MAXINE. Oh, no, he doesn't mean that!

PHILIP. Doesn't mean *what?*

MAXINE. His wife's flipped her lid.

ADDISON. She has?

PHILIP. She hasn't! Miss Threadgill, I wish you wouldn't—

MAXINE. I meant that he was going to *say* she flipped her lid, and that wasn't what you meant.

ADDISON. Then what *did* he mean? He said she was all right physically, but—

PHILIP. But what?

ADDISON. Damn it, Philip, that's what *I'm* trying to ask *you!* (NORA *enters from kitchen.*)

NORA. Did somebody want a drink?

ADDISON. I didn't, but I do now! Bring me a brandy, Nora, please.

MAXINE. What would *you* like, Doctor? Whatever it is, I'll get it.

PHILIP. (*Icily.*) *Lockjaw!*

NORA. (*At bar.*) We're fresh out. What's your second choice?

PHILIP. I'll have a brandy, too, Nora, thank you.

ADDISON. Philip—what about Winifred's *mind?!*

PHILIP. Now, calm yourself, Addison. Your wife's mind is perfectly fine. It's her current mental *mood* I was going to refer to. She needs a large dose of self-confidence. I want you to humor her.

ADDISON. She's free to do anything she wants, right now . . . ?

PHILIP. Anything?

ADDISON. Well—anything within reason, I mean.

PHILIP. Ah, but that's exactly what I *don't* mean. When I say anything, I *mean* anything. Never mind whether you think it's *reasonable* or not. (NORA *joins them with two glasses of brandy, during:*)

ADDISON. But surely, Philip—

PHILIP. Believe me, Addison, Winifred has had a great shock. (NORA *arrives; they take glasses.*) Thank you, Nora.

NORA. (*To* MAXINE.) Can I get you anything?

MAXINE. A tetanus shot.

PHILIP. Miss Threadgill, why don't you take a stroll around the grounds? As long as you're going to be staying on here awhile, you may as well know where everything is.

NORA. Come on, dearie. I'll show you the way.

MAXINE. Well . . . All right, thank you. (*She allows* NORA *to lead her out through patio doors.*)

PHILIP. (*Man to man:*) That's the curse of being a

doctor. Every spinster in a starched cap thinks she belongs forever at your side! When I take a wife, I want to make beautiful music, not medical history!

ADDISON. Philip, we were speaking of *my* wife, and her mental state. You assured me the operation was relatively simple . . .

PHILIP. And it is. But its implications are not. You see, Addison, at the moment, Winifred may feel that she's —well—that she's no longer a *woman.*

ADDISON. I see. Yes, I see. But surely there are limits to this humoring?

PHILIP. Well, naturally, you hold off a bit if she asks for a champagne glass and a bottle of cyanide. But anything harmless—even if it may seem a bit—oh—

ADDISON. Screwy?

PHILIP. Exactly. You must try to be—*flexible,* Addison. Give a little. Just for a week or so. And you'll see that Winifred will be— (*Stops as* LORELEI *and* WINIFRED *enter from kitchen.*)

LORELEI. I've got to go. My nephew is staying with me, and he'll be wanting his dinner soon. Could you give me a lift, Doctor Morgan? I came here on foot.

WINIFRED. I had no idea you lived so close by . . .

LORELEI. Just a hop and a skip over the hill. You'll be seeing lots of me!

WINIFRED. (*Quietly.*) Terrific.

LORELEI. I knew you'd be pleased! Oh, I'm forgetting that pamphlet! (*Plumps herself down on sofa, her huge purse before her on table, rummages as she talks.*) I know it's in here someplace. I never throw anything away. (*During next part of speech, she removes in turn and places on the table a great number of disparate items: a pair of tennis sneakers, a garish-covered novel, a large box of chocolates, a small crowbar, and a medium-sized teddy bear, one item per asterisk:*) I think a woman in your condition (*) is unwise to simply let herself pine away. (*) If I can— Whoops, there goes my diet! (*) If I can help you readjust (*) to the world after your

long and grim struggle (*) I won't count the cost of—
Darn! Where has it gotten to—?

PHILIP. Could you use a larger table?

LORELEI. (*Laughs.*) No, no, if they fall, they fall. Don't know why I carry so much junk around with me, but you never know when you're going to need— (*The rest is lost as she literally plunges her head and arms inside purse to rummage further.*)

WINIFRED. Lorelei considers a day ill-spent if she doesn't do some generous meddling in another person's life. It's the secret of her charm.

ADDISON. Her *charm?*

WINIFRED. I *said* it was a *secret*, Addison!

PHILIP. (*To* ADDISON:) Speaking of charm— Where's Bonnie?

WINIFRED. Frankly, Philip, I think she's avoiding you.

ADDISON. (*Blustering over her bluntness.*) Well, Philip, you know women!

WINIFRED. That's probably *why* she's avoiding you.

PHILIP. I assure you, Addison, I've never given Bonnie cause to—

ADDISON. Naturally not! Bonnie just—mistrusts her emotions about you.

PHILIP. Then she *has* emotions about me? I find that encouraging.

WINIFRED. Don't.

PHILIP. What does she have against me, anyway?

WINIFRED. It's this way, Philip— A woman wants a man to be intrigued by her—to find her a mysterious, provocative enigma. You, on the other hand, are a gynecologist.

LORELEI. (*Pops head out of purse, waves rubber-banded sheaf of odd-sized pamphets aloft.*) I *knew* it was in here someplace! (*Slips off band, starts sorting for proper pamphlet, during:*) Now let's see—I recall there was a young girl on the cover, on her knees, sort of hunching forward . . . (*PHONE rings;* ADDISON *gets it.*)

ADDISON. Hello, Titan Incorporated—! . . . Oh, **yes,** certainly. (*Holds out phone.*) Philip, it's for you.

PHILIP. (*Taking phone.*) My answering service never sleeps! I wish a doctor could go places without being on constant call . . . (*He and* ADDISON *remain by desk, as* PHILIP *pantomimes speaking over phone, during:*)

LORELEI. (*Squinting at pamphlet myopically.*) Here— is that a girl on her knees, Winifred?

WINIFRED. (*Watching men, gives brief glance.*) What? . . . Oh, yes, it is, Lorelei. (*Turns back toward men, during:*)

LORELEI. Thank heaven! (*Places pamphlet on table beside bowl, starts replacing other items in purse, during:*) Now, don't be discouraged at the outset. Yoga exercises look a lot harder than they actually are. It's just the thing you need to get your muscles toned up again.

PHILIP. (*Hangs up phone, on:*) Got to see a patient. Probably just a bellyache, but you never know. Coming, Lorelei?

LORELEI. Just soon as I get all this mess back into the bag . . .

ADDISON. Just a moment, Philip. My daughter should pay her respects. (*Shouts:*) Bonnie! Come out here this instant!

BONNIE. (*Steps in from kitchen.*) You shrieked, Father?

ADDISON. Don't be facetious. I want you to say goodbye to our guests.

BONNIE. (*Amicably flippant.*) Goodbye, guests!

ADDISON. Oh, what's the use!

PHILIP. You're looking well, Bonnie.

BONNIE. *Thank* you, sir!

ADDISON. Now, Bonnie—

BONNIE. I'm sorry, Philip, really I am. Dad just puts me on the defensive. I'd probably be much more sociable if he didn't keep insisting on it. Nice to see you.

WINIFRED. When she was a child, he used to have her

recite poems at the guests. It left scars. (*All look up as* NORA *and* MAXINE *enter from patio.*)

ADDISON. Finished the tour so soon?

NORA. Miss Threadgill got squeamish. I should never have mentioned the Headless Horseman.

MAXINE. This is a spooky neighborhood. And it gets dark as night as soon as you step off the lawn into the woods.

PHILIP. That's right, this is Washington Irving country, isn't it!

LORELEI. (*Purse packed, rises.*) The Tarrytown folks still keep his home, Sunnyside, as a kind of museum. I hope you don't miss it, nurse.

MAXINE. (*Shivers.*) Not a bit!

PHILIP. Well, I have an impatient patient, so— (*Starts out.*)

LORELEI. (*Following.*) Winifred, you *will* read the pamphlet carefully and consider it, won't you?

WINIFRED. Every word. (*They exit.*)

BONNIE. (*Notices* MAXINE *is shivering.*) Miss Threadgill, would you like a brandy?

MAXINE. Oh, I never drink on duty. Scout's honor—I mean, nurse's oath.

WINIFRED. Would you like to go off duty?

MAXINE. A person trained in the field of medicine is never off duty.

NORA. You must have a rotten union!

MAXINE. I mean, once you're a nurse, you're *always* a nurse. There are some things time never changes.

ADDISON. Sort of like "always a bridesmaid," isn't it! (MAXINE *suddenly covers her face, drops onto the sofa, and sobs.*)

WINIFRED. Addison—!

BONNIE. (*Heads for bar.*) I'll get her a brandy.

ADDISON. (*Dumbfounded.*) What did I *say?*

WINIFRED. It's what Doctor Morgan *didn't* say! (*To* MAXINE:) There-there, it's all right, dear.

ADDISON. *What's* all right?

MAXINE. (*Burbling miserably.*) I've given him four years of my life! Passing out pills, taking temperatures, giving shots— Why do I do it? Why!

NORA. Excuse me, Miss Threadgill, but—are you independently wealthy?

MAXINE. (*Blinks, at sea.*) No . . . ?

NORA. Then *that's* why.

BONNIE. (*Pouring a brandy at bar.*) Nora, she means the devotion, not the working hours.

WINIFRED. (*To* ADDISON.) I *told* you I didn't like Doctor Morgan.

BONNIE. I can't imagine why Miss Threadgill does!

MAXINE. B-but— He's the only single doctor I *know!*

(WALDO LENNIMER *appears on the patio; he is thin, thirtyish, quivering with rage, and clutching two gladiolas; just as* BONNIE *steps from behind the bar with the glass of brandy, he steps majestically across the doorsill, and brandishes the gladiolas wildly at her, on:*)

WALDO. (*Biting off each word.*) You forgot *these!* (*Slams flowers onto floor.*)

BONNIE. (*Stares, then realizes who this is, averts her face from his, and says more wearily than sarcastically:*) Doctor Lennimer, I presume?

WALDO. (*Almost sobbing.*) How could you!? How could you do such a terrible thing?! Why did you do it? (*WINIFRED and* MAXINE—*the latter having reacted to* WALDO's *title, and busily drying her eyes with the hem of her cape—have risen, now, and along with* ADDISON *and* NORA *stare at this unexpected visitor, trying to follow his meaning.*)

BONNIE. It was all a mistake. I thought they were quite pretty—

WALDO. They *are* pretty!

BONNIE. *That* wasn't my mistake. I meant picking them. I thought that was *our* garden.

WALDO. (*Not quite hysterical, but close.*) Didn't you see me waving?

BONNIE. I thought you were being neighborly.

WALDO. (*Hysterical.*) Neighborly?!

BONNIE. (*Hands him glass of brandy.*) Here.

WALDO. (*Takes it suspiciously.*) What is it?

BONNIE. Just what the doctor ordered. Drink up, it'll help you settle down.

WALDO. I don't *want* to settle down! I'll *never* settle down!

MAXINE. Doctors are all alike.

BONNIE. Oh, excuse me. Doctor Lennimer . . . Nurse Threadgill.

WALDO. Are you this maniac's keeper?

MAXINE. (*Indicates* WINIFRED.) No, this one.

WALDO. They're *both* nuts?

ADDISON. Now see here, my good man—! (GUNTHER *enters from patio, cap on head, empty sandwich plate in one hand.*)

GUNTHER. Horseshoe's up! What's next?

NORA. Can you unpack bone china without breaking it?

GUNTHER. There's one way to find out! (*Exits to kitchen.*)

NORA. Oh, dear! Excuse me— (*Exits after him.*)

WALDO. *Horseshoe?!*

MAXINE. Gesundheit!

ADDISON. Bonnie, did you tell Mister Chowdy to nail it open end up?

BONNIE. What's the difference?

ADDISON. You don't want all the good luck to run out the open end.

WALDO. Good grief—they're *all* nuts!

ADDISON. My good man, I am Addison Flinder, president of Titan, Incorporated! (*When* WALDO *fails to react, adds a questioning mental nudge:*) . . . Products for *Men*—?

WALDO. Aren't you sure?

ADDISON. (*Icily.*) I'd better check on that horseshoe! (*Exits through foyer, during:*)

BONNIE. Now, Doctor Lennimer, about my little mistake—

WALDO. Little?! The judges are coming by on Saturday, and what are they going to see? Five yards of green stumps! (NORA *enters from kitchen, during:*)

WINIFRED. What judges, Doctor Lennimer?

WALDO. For the summer gardeners' competition, of course! I've won two years running. One more win and the silver cup would be permanently mine. But now—! (*Shrugs miserably, drains glass, chokes.*) What—what was *in* that, anyhow?

BONNIE. Hennessy Bras d'Or. Cognac. You're supposed to take small sips.

MAXINE. Why?

WINIFRED. It's forty-eight dollars a bottle.

WALDO. *How* did you people get into *my* neighborhood?!

NORA. We just followed the yellow brick road.

MAXINE. Oh, Doctor, can't anything be done for your garden?

WALDO. How are you fixed for green bandaids?!

BONNIE. Now, wait a minute, Doctor—I didn't take *all* the flowers.

WALDO. Just the *best* ones!

WINIFRED. Couldn't you buy some potted gladiolas and transplant them? I'd to glad to cover the cost.

WALDO. You think I'd have *strange* flowers in *my* garden?!

NORA. I wouldn't be a bit surprised. (*As he reacts, she turns to* WINIFRED.) How many will there be for dinner, Mrs. Flinder?

WINIFRED. Let me think . . .

MAXINE. Doctor— Do you practice around here?

WALDO. Every day. Otherwise my fingers get stiff.

MAXINE. *That* makes sense.

WINIFRED. (*Finishes estimate.*) I guess four, Nora. The

family and Miss Threadgill . . . Oh! Would *you* care to join us, Doctor Lennimer?

BONNIE. Yes, please do! What's your absolute top favorite dish?

WALDO. Roast Long Island duckling with orange rum-sauce and wild rice.

WINIFRED. Nora—?

NORA. I can manage the orange.

WALDO. No, thank you.

BONNIE. There must be something we can do for you. I feel so terrible—

WALDO. I really couldn't think of eating, anyhow. When I think about that cup, and this coming Saturday—!

MAXINE. Couldn't you rearrange the other flowers to fill in where these came out?

WALDO. Why—I don't know . . . I never thought of that . . .

MAXINE. I'll bet you could do it! With skilled fingers like yours—!

WALDO. Do you really think so, Miss—? I didn't quite catch your name . . .

MAXINE. Miss Threadgill, R.N. But you can call me Maxine!

WALDO. I wonder . . .

MAXINE. Come on. Try it. There's still plenty of daylight left.

WALDO. All right. (*Squares shoulders.*) Maxine.

MAXINE. I meant rearranging the flowers, Doctor Lennimer.

WALDO. Please call me Waldo.

MAXINE. Is that your name?

WINIFRED. Of course it is, Miss Threadgill! Now, you two young people just run along, and don't worry about me.

MAXINE. Oh, could I? I'd love to help out. I could pass him the instruments! (*Takes* WALDO's *arm, starts to lead him out through patio doors.*)

BONNIE. Don't forget to sterilize the trowels.

WALDO. (*Over shoulder, as* MAXINE *leads him out.*) What in the world for? Oh, I'm taking your glass! (*Hands it back to* BONNIE.)

BONNIE. (*Taking it.*) I would have trusted you.

ADDISON. (*Entering through foyer.*) I knew it! I knew it! Open end down! (*Crosses to kitchen past* NORA, *exits during:*)

NORA. If there's going to be a fight, I'd better look after the china! (*Exits to kitchen.*)

WALDO. Is your husband so very superstitious?

WINIFRED. He just wants us to match the local atmosphere. A horseshoe is supposed to bring luck.

MAXINE. Good or bad?

BONNIE. It depends how you hang it. I wonder what would happen if you put it up sideways?

WALDO. You'd probably get half and half— Like inheriting a lot of money when a loved one died.

MAXINE. Don't talk about death. It's bad luck.

WINIFRED. Why, Miss Threadgill! You are the last person I would have thought would be superstitious.

MAXINE. Oh, I'm not superstitious— (*Raps folding door twice.*) —knock on wood—I just don't believe in taking chances.

GUNTHER. (*Enters from kitchen trailed by* ADDISON.) I tell you, I *did* nail it open end up! It must have slipped and pivoted around.

ADDISON. I suppose the *brownies* came and moved it when you weren't looking! (*They exit through foyer, on:*)

GUNTHER. In this neighborhood, I wouldn't be surprised!

MAXINE. *I* used to be a Brownie.

BONNIE. I don't think Dad meant that kind.

WALDO. The woman who used to live here was a den mother, or something. Everyplace you looked—little *people!* I almost bought a dog. But a dog would be harder on the flower bed than they would.

MAXINE. That reminds me— Shouldn't we be going? The sun won't stay up forever.

WALDO. Good idea. I want the transplant traces gone by Saturday.

MAXINE. See you later! (*She and* WALDO *exit through patio.*)

WINIFRED. (*Goes to sit on sofa, during:*) I could have sworn your father said this was a new house. But if there was a former owner—I guess not.

BONNIE. (*Returning glass to bar, refills her own.*) Well, Dad had it fixed up quite a bit. New paint and plaster and stuff. That's probably what he meant. (*Comes to sit beside* WINIFRED *on:*) It was an awfully long two weeks without you. I missed you.

WINIFRED. I missed you, too, dear.

BONNIE. Were you very, very sick? I was so worried when you weren't allowed any visitors . . . (*HAMMER-ING sounds off Left.*)

WINIFRED. (*Looks off Left, hesitates, then comes to a decision and turns back to* BONNIE.) . . . Can you keep a secret, dear?

BONNIE. A secret—?

WINIFRED. I'm just bursting to tell somebody. I thought it would be easy, but when you've done something terrible, it weighs on you until you let it out.

BONNIE. Now-now, Mother. *You*—do something *terrible?* I find that hard to believe.

WINIFRED. But I did, darling, I did. And it's haunting me.

BONNIE. That's just the operation talking. When you're all rested up—

WINIFRED. But Bonnie—that's just it . . . I haven't *had* an operation!

BONNIE. (*Half-rises.*) Uh—listen, Mother— Doctor Morgan must be back in town by now. Why don't I phone him and—

WINIFRED. Darling, your mother is not the least bit nuts.

BONNIE. Nobody said you were! But I know it's been an emotional strain on you, and—

WINIFRED. Bonnie, dearest— Doctor Morgan and I cooked up this whole thing together! Don't you see? It's your *father* who needs the rest! (BONNIE *slowly settles down again.*) Doctor Morgan's been telling him to slow down for years.

BONNIE. Mother—you did a dreadful thing!

WINIFRED. But darling, how *else* could I get your father out of the city? Could anything but a dire emergency ever pry him out of his precious office? I know it's a deceitful lie, but I'd hardly call it *dreadful* . . .

BONNIE. I don't mean the lie—I mean that "Camille" act you were pulling when you walked in here! (*Does frail, timid quaver:*) "What *is* this place? . . . Where have you *brought* me?" You should be ashamed of yourself!

WINIFRED. You're mixing your sick heroines. That wasn't Camille—that was Ophelia.

BONNIE. I thought Ophelia sang old ballads and passed out rosemary.

WINIFRED. Well, I had to draw the line somewhere!

BONNIE. Mother, I think it's a simply marvelous scheme. A house in the country is just what Dad needs. All at once, I don't even mind the moose!

WINIFRED. *I* do. Do you remember Grandmother Flinder?

BONNIE. Nora said the same thing . . .

WINIFRED. Dear Nora! (*Looks toward moosehead.*) I can't quite place where the resemblance lies—maybe it's that glassy look in the eyes.

BONNIE. Well, I hope it's not the *ears!* (*Raises her glass.*) Here's happy days to all of us.

WINIFRED. Especially to your poor overworked father! (*Both drink; then:*)

BONNIE. Mother—I just thought—if you weren't in the hospital the past two weeks—where *were* you?

WINIFRED. I went to Paris.

BONNIE. *Paris?* You mean, *the* Paris? We were just there last summer.

WINIFRED. I thought it might be fun to try it for once without your father along. And it was. I don't know what those Frenchmen have got, but if they could bottle it, they'd put your father right out of business!

BONNIE. Wasn't the trip kind of expensive?

WINIFRED. It was a lot cheaper than a two-week hospital bill! Do you know what they charge per day for a semi-private room—?!

ADDISON. (*Just entering through foyer, trailed by* GUNTHER.) Now, Winifred, you mustn't trouble yourself about things like that. Put your mind at ease. I've already sent a check for the full amount to Doctor Morgan.

BONNIE. And he *took* it?!

ADDISON. I beg your pardon—?

BONNIE. Oh, nothing, Dad—nothing.

WINIFRED. You should have let *me* handle that, Addison. I like to check all the items on the bill.

ADDISON. I'm sure Doctor Morgan is an honest man.

WINIFRED. Still—I wish you'd let me deal with Doctor Morgan myself.

ADDISON. I thought you didn't like Doctor Morgan?

WINIFRED. I don't. More than ever.

GUNTHER. Excuse me—I'd better get out and help Mrs. Larkin with that china. Unless there's something else you wanted me to do?

ADDISON. As a matter of fact, there is. I saw a spot out back of the house would make a wonderful putting green . . . (*Leads* GUNTHER *toward patio.*) Let me show you the spot. I think the lawnmower has adjustable blades, and if you can cut the grass down short enough— (*He and* GUNTHER *have exited out of sight and earshot through patio.*)

BONNIE. The nerve of Doctor Morgan, taking that money from Dad!

WINIFRED. Addison may only have sent the check today. Perhaps Doctor Morgan simply hasn't gotten it yet. Let's wait a few days.

BONNIE. And then?

WINIFRED. (*Rises, speaks quietly.*) Then I am going to be so mad my gaze will wither any growing thing! (*Sees* WALDO'S *flung-down gladiolas on floor.*) I think I've started already! (*Picks them up, fluffs them a bit, comes down to place them with others on table, during:*)

BONNIE. (*Going to bar to replace brandy bottle, etc.*) Did I hear Lorelei mention her nephew Tony?

WINIFRED. Yes. He's staying with her while he writes his doctorate paper. Must be jolly fun for the two of them. He's probably doing a case history of *her*.

BONNIE. What's he studying to be, a dietician?

WINIFRED. No, a psychiatrist. Lorelei plans to bring him around soon.

BONNIE. I didn't know he passed out.

WINIFRED. Really, Bonnie, you should watch those flippant answers. They're going to get you in trouble some day.

BONNIE. They did today. I thought our handyman was going to bite me.

WINIFRED. (*Straightens from flower-arranging, surveys results, shrugs resignedly.*) It would have served you right. What do you want to be brittle and sophisticated for, anyhow?

BONNIE. It comes of working for Dad. The people he deals with aren't quite the kind of men I want to attract. No matter how you slice it, we're in the perfume business.

WINIFRED. There's nothing wrong with a man looking and smelling nice.

BONNIE. I have nothing against the users—it's those inventors! You can imagine what kind of man gets in a snit over the comparative allures of pine oil and sandalwood!

WINIFRED. Bonnie, you're speaking of the man I love.

BONNIE. (*Comes down to her.*) It's different with Dad. If it sells, who cares how it smells! When he worries, it's about the dollars—

WINIFRED. (*Finishing the familiar phrase:*) —when

they worry, it's about the scents! Your father made that joke up before you were born.

BONNIE. He's been in business an awfully long time . . .

WINIFRED. That's precisely why I intend to get him out of it. It's not as though we need money, anymore. We've put plenty away.

BONNIE. It won't last long if you keep hopping over to Paris every time the fancy takes you.

WINIFRED. That reminds me! Would you be good for twenty dollars till tomorrow?

BONNIE. For twenty dollars, I'd be good for a week!

WINIFRED. I hope Mister Chowdy *does* bite you. What does it take to get a straight answer from my own daughter?

BONNIE. Certainly not a crooked mother.

WINIFRED. (*Throws up her hands in surrender.*) I give up! (*Rises.*) I think I'll see what Nora *is* preparing for dinner. Doctor Lennimer's favorite menu is making me hungry!

BONNIE. Do you think it's wise to eat hearty during your convalescence?

WINIFRED. I plan to nibble at the table, while your father's watching.

BONNIE. Then I'll distract him, while you gorge.

WINIFRED. That's my girl! . . . Seriously, though, I'll have to practice my symptoms. I have to hover just on the verge of cyclothymia—that's a kind of ups-and-downs emotionalism. I looked it up.

BONNIE. Thank heaven for Doctor Morgan and has medical library! Always select a conspirator who knows how to read.

WINIFRED. (*Starting for kitchen.*) I do hope I'm wrong about Doctor Morgan and that check. I may have to switch to our neighbor for medical care.

BONNIE. I suppose you could, if you come unstrung. (WINIFRED *looks a question.*) He's a piano teacher, Mother. Doctor of Musicology.

WINIFRED. I wonder—do you suppose Miss Threadgill knows?

BONNIE. Come to think of it— She *was* rather adoring for a dedicated woman.

WINIFRED. Well, we'd better set the poor girl straight before she proposes. She could *never* hold *his* instrument on a tray! (*Exits to kitchen. Left alone,* BONNIE *stretches, then abruptly looks at her watch, nods briskly, goes to telephone, dials, and stands facing downstage waiting for a response; then:*)

BONNIE. (*On phone.*) Hello—Doctor Morgan? Bonnie Flinder . . . Fine, just fine. So is Mother . . . That's what I'm calling about . . . I think you *do* know what I mean, Doctor! A small matter of a check—? (*Behind her, unnoticed,* ADDISON *enters through patio doors, en route to bar; he stops when he hears* BONNIE *continue:*) All I know, Doctor Morgan, is that you seem to be practicing a bit of deception on my father! . . . If you don't tell him the truth, I will. . . . No, Mother is calm right now, but in a few days she is going to be quite mad! . . . (ADDISON *reacts with horror, fingertips going to his temples; he lurches backward through patio doors, incredulous, remains at entrance to hear:*) You wouldn't *dare* tell Dad the truth! There's such a thing as a privileged communication, Doctor! If you tell him about Mother, I'll tell the world you're not to be trusted with a patient's secrets! . . . Well, that's better . . . (ADDISON, *stunned and shaken, whirls and exits across patio.*) Yes, bring us the check, and we'll tear it up and say no more about it . . . Thank you, Doctor. Good day! (*Hangs up triumphantly, dusts hands, starts toward kitchen.*) Mother—?

WINIFRED. (*Enters.*) Nora's going to whip some kind of dinner up as soon as she gets the rest of the dishes put away.

BONNIE. I called Doctor Morgan. He got the check, all right! I made him promise to bring it by, so we can destroy it.

WINIFRED. But, darling, we can't do that! It must be cashed.

BONNIE. I never thought of that! You're right. If Dad doesn't get a cancelled check from the bank, he'll find out everything.

WINIFRED. Well, we'll just have Doctor Morgan sign it, and we can go with him when he presents it at the bank, and get the money.

BONNIE. But—then—won't we be robbing Dad?

WINIFRED. Not really. I'll use it to replace the money I spent from my allowance to take that Paris trip, and everything comes out even.

BONNIE. How do you figure? You end up with a free trip to Paris, with Dad footing the bill.

WINIFRED. After twenty-five years of marriage, it's the least he could do. (ADDISON *enters with* GUNTHER *through patio, on:*)

BONNIE. Mother, there's something wrong with your logic!

ADDISON. (*Instantly, too heartily:*) *Nonsense!* (WOMEN *and* GUNTHER *react.*) Her mind is fine! Just fine!

BONNIE. I never said it wasn't . . .

ADDISON. (*A* sotto voce *growl, as if* WINIFRED *couldn't hear it:*) You were coming mighty *close!*

WINIFRED. Addison, you really shouldn't go out in the sun without a hat.

ADDISON. I *never* wear a hat— (*Remembers to "humor" her:*) But I'll get one! I promise! We'll *all* get hats.

GUNTHER. I've *got* a hat.

ADDISON. Have *two!* (MAXINE *and* WALDO *enter from patio.*)

BONNIE. Well, hello there! How did it go?

MAXINE. It was wonderful! We went all over the bed together!

WALDO. I'm a cinch to win the loving cup, now! (AD-DISON *reacts.*)

MAXINE. Waldo has the most delicate touch—

WALDO. Maxine's not so bad herself! I like a woman who's not afraid to get her hands dirty.

ADDISON. Doctor Lennimer! There are ladies present!

WINIFRED. Addison, what's come over you?

ADDISON. Didn't you hear what they said?!

WINIFRED. They're all set for the annual competition . . .

GUNTHER. Mrs. Gullock's entered this year. She's counting on me to help her win.

ADDISON. Mister Chowdy—!

BONNIE. Before my father has a stroke, will somebody please say "flowers"?

ADDISON. *Flowers?!*

BONNIE. Thanks, Dad.

WINIFRED. Miss Threadgill, I've been very disturbed about something—

ADDISON. Nonsense! You're perfectly normal. Fight it, Winifred, fight with all your might!

WINIFRED. What *are* you *talking* about, Addison? I just want to tell her Waldo is a piano teacher.

ADDISON. Of course he is! (*Nods vigorously at* WALDO *to* "*go along.*") Isn't that right, doctor?!

WALDO. (*Bewildered but honest.*) Uh—absolutely.

MAXINE. (*Genuinely going along with it.*) Uh—*naturally* he's a piano teacher. *Lots* of doctors are . . .

WINIFRED. Then you *did* know? Oh, I'm so glad. I feel much better, now.

BONNIE. (*Sensing something, but unsure what.*) Dad—excuse me, but—how are *you* feeling at the moment. . . ?

ADDISON. *Fine! Tiptop! Never better!* Stop *asking* me things!

WINIFRED. Why are you shouting so?

ADDISON. (*Ultra-softly:*) I'm not shouting.

WALDO. Would you all like to come and see what Maxine and I were doing?

ADDISON. Haven't you done enough?!

BONNIE. Dad, I don't think you understand. Doctor

Lennimer was upset, and Miss Threadgill simply wanted to help him cover the bare spots— (*Realizes this is no help.*) Forget it.

GUNTHER. She means helping him in the garden.

ADDISON. What does Miss Threadgill know about gardening?

WINIFRED. Oh, that's right— You didn't know she was a Brownie.

ADDISON. (*Goggle-eyed, but "humoring."*) Of course I did! We all know. A tiny little creature that goes around helping folks.

BONNIE. (*Sensing his drift.*) Dad, maybe *you'd* better take a nice nap, hm? You'll need your strength if Lorelei drops by again. She may bring Tony, too.

ADDISON. Say, isn't he a psychiatrist?

BONNIE. Well, he's on the verge.

ADDISON. That's *good* . . . Yes, indeed. That's *very* good . . . Just perfect . . . (ADDISON's *mind is obviously laboring over something, but the others are discomfitted too much by his attitude to stick around and ask questions, so:*)

WINIFRED. (*Starts for stairs.*) You know, I think I *will* take a little nap before dinner—

MAXINE. (*Starts after her.*) I'll help you get settled, Mrs. Flinder.

WALDO. And I have a customer coming. The little Miller boy from across the way. He's having a dreadful time with scales.

MAXINE. The main thing is to keep him from scratching. (*She exits up stairs after* WINIFRED, *while* WALDO *looks blankly on.*)

WALDO. (*To* BONNIE, *after a moment:*) He *does* tend to fidget a bit . . . (*Exits via patio.*)

GUNTHER. Guess I'll go see if Nora needs a hand with anything. (*Starts for kitchen.*)

BONNIE. I think you can help put away the dishes for her—she has a dinner to whip up.

GUNTHER. I'll remind her. (*Exits to kitchen.*)

ADDISON. Now, young lady, you and I are going to have a talk!

BONNIE. (*Uneasy before his secretive manner.*) Why— sure, Dad. What about?

ADDISON. Do you mind if I fix myself a drink? I've had a rather severe shock.

BONNIE. You know, I *thought* there was something— Go ahead— No, better yet, you sit down on the sofa, and I'll fix one for *both* of us.

ADDISON. I— Yes, I think I will. Thank you, dear. Make it something strong. (*He sits, she goes to bar and fixes, during:*)

BONNIE. Will do. Meantime, you tell me what's got you so upset.

ADDISON. Was I that obvious?

BONNIE. Only to one who knows you well—namely, me. You *always* tend to *rumble* like a volcano . . . but I thought I detected a few *eruptions,* today . . . What's it all about?

ADDISON. I know the truth about your mother.

BONNIE. I—I don't know what you mean, Dad . . .

ADDISON. Bonnie, I admire your loyalty, but you can drop the pretense. I overhead you talking.

BONNIE. Oh, dear! Mother will be terribly upset—

ADDISON. No, I don't think so. They say that people who lose their minds enjoy being that way. It's the on-lookers who suffer.

BONNIE. Hold on, you just lost me. Who's losing *whose* mind?

ADDISON. Don't pretend. Let's be honest with one an-other. Your mother is quietly going off her trolley.

BONNIE. (*About to bring drinks down to sofa, freezes, shocked.*) You're wrong, Dad! She's perfectly sound . . .

ADDISON. I know what I heard.

BONNIE. What *did* you hear . . . ? (*Both react guiltily as* NORA *abruptly steps in from kitchen.*)

NORA. I can't fix that dinner up. The blender doesn't

work. Neither does the refrigerator, the lights, or the electric can-opener.

ADDISON. It's probably the main switch in the fuse box hasn't been turned on! Tell Mister Chowdy to take care of it!

NORA. You don't have to bite my head off! (*Exits to kitchen, on:*) You'd be the first to complain if I couldn't mix your Sippy Powders!

BONNIE. Oh, Dad—! Is your ulcer acting up again?

ADDISON. Never mind my stomach! We're discussing your mother's head!

BONNIE. (*Comes to sofa, sits with him, hands over his drink, during:*) There's nothing *wrong* with Mother's head!

ADDISON. I *know* she's sane right *now!* It's a *few days* from now that's breaking my heart. One night she'll be fine—the next morning she'll wake up gaga!

BONNIE. Dad, you're *wrong!* Mother is absolutely normal!

ADDISON. I eavesdropped on your call to Doctor Morgan. (BONNIE *reacts.*) You said he'd deceived me. You said that in a few days, your mother would be mad!

BONNIE. (*Realizes, aghast.*) I did say that, didn't I!

ADDISON. It was all horribly clear. What *else* could the doctor be deceiving me about? (*Smiles wanly at her.*)

BONNIE. (*Trapped, smiles wanly back.*) What else, indeed! (*Clinks glasses with him.*) Happy days! (*Drains her drink.*)

ADDISON. (*After only a token sip of drink.*) Tell me— exactly—how long before her mind is gone?

BONNIE. (*Squirming, trying to think.*) Oh . . . there's no telling. Maybe, though, if we—uh—just treat her right, she may *never* go—um—over the hill . . .

ADDISON. Bonnie, are you blind? She's halfway down the slope! (BONNIE *rises to replenish her drink, and he lets himself slide sideways to a mournful reclining position, on:*) She thinks Lennimer is a piano teacher. She said Miss Threadgill was a brownie.

BONNIE. You're lucky she didn't tell you this house used to be a *meeting*-place for Brownies!

ADDISON. (*Groans, covers his eyes.*) She believes *that?*

BONNIE. (*Behind bar, now.*) Of course she does. You see, Dad—

(*Before she can explain, two things happen:* WINIFRED, *now in a frilly lavender nightgown and peignoir, comes sailing down the stairs, doesn't see* ADDISON *on the sofa—he is concealed by its back and his recumbent position—and twinkletoes her way gracefully across the stage toward Downstage Right, arms extended to trail the open peignoir like butterfly wings. The second thing that happens is that* GUNTHER *enters from kitchen during the last syllable of her line, and has to clutch her at the waist to avert a collision, so that she comes to a startled stop, arms still out at shoulder height, something like a wanton flaunting her wares. The run, the stop, and the two following speeches all occur within about three seconds:*)

WINIFRED. (*Gaily, during cross:*) Darling! Look what I picked up yesterday in *Paris!*

GUNTHER. (*Clutching her waist.*) Where do you keep your fuse box?

ADDISON. (*Sitting up and seeing them.*) *Yesterday* in *Paris—?!*

BONNIE. (*Raises her glass at bar.*) You're right, Dad. She *is* nuts! (WINIFRED *and* GUNTHER *remain in open-armed and clutch stances, staring wide-eyed at one another;* ADDISON *groans, covers his eyes, and sinks back recumbent onto sofa, and* BONNIE *shuts her eyes and stoically drains her glass, as—*)

THE CURTAIN FALLS

ACT TWO

Curtain-rise finds the FLINDER *home much the same as before, except that through the open patio doors the sylvan backdrop is nearly invisible thanks to enveloping darkness, though the patio area itself can be seen in the spill of light from the interior of the house. It is shortly after sunset—somewhere between seven and eight P.M.* BONNIE *and* WINIFRED *are each seated in the center of one of the two sections of the sofa, so that there is a bit of space between them. Both are leaning back, arms folded, legs straight out before them, crossed at the ankles. They seem weary—not sleepy, but exhausted. At curtain-rise, they do not immediately speak, each apparently deep in unhappy thought. Then, after a moment,* WINIFRED—*still in her nightgown and peignoir—takes a deep breath and expels it in a long, slow sigh. This brings* BONNIE *back out of her reverie, and she turns her head to look inquiringly at her mother.*

WINIFRED. (*Without looking at* BONNIE.) Addison could at least have let me get dressed for dinner. I've never felt so silly in my life. Nora nearly dropped the mashed potatoes when she saw me.

BONNIE. It's not Dad's fault. I think he's trying to humor you. If you want to romp around in a state of undress, it's his duty to be big about it.

WINIFRED. But I *told* him I wanted to get my clothes on!

BONNIE. You also said you got the outfit yesterday in Paris. He didn't believe that, either—thank heaven!

WINIFRED. I should thank heaven your father thinks I'm a fruitcake?

BONNIE. Mother, I *had* to tell him that. Only a fruit-cake takes mythical trips to Paris. If you hadn't come galloping in like queen of the May—! How can you ever face Mister Chowdy again?!

WINIFRED. Certainly not as "Mister Chowdy." After that mad embrace, I'll have to call him by his given name. He can call me "Winnie."

BONNIE. Then pretty soon, secret meetings, cocktails for two, discovery, a juicy scandal—!

WINIFRED. And all because the blender didn't work.

BONNIE. (*Stands up, stretches.*) Well, the lights are on, so I assume he finally found the fusebox.

WINIFRED. With trembling hands. (BONNIE *looks at her; she explains:*) I was also wearing French perfume. You probably missed it when Nora brought on the liver and onions. Can you smell it now?

BONNIE. (*Inhales.*) You must have spent a bundle. How did you get home—hitch a ride?

WINIFRED. I vamped an airline pilot. They get very lonely up in the clouds. (NORA *enters from kitchen.*)

NORA. Mrs. Flinder—aren't you dressed yet? There'll be men at the party.

WINIFRED. What's the point? It's almost my bedtime, anyhow. (*Belatedly reacts.*) *What* party?

NORA. Your welcome-home party. Didn't Mister Flinder tell you?

WINIFRED. (*Stands up quickly.*) No, he most certainly did not! What in the world was Addison thinking of?!

BONNIE. In French perfume, you can ask?

NORA. I'm sorry—I didn't know you hadn't been told. Now I don't know *what* to do . . .

WINIFRED. Now, don't worry, Nora. Perhaps a party is a good idea. Addison might overcome his suspicions if I'm bright, witty and vivacious for our guests.

BONNIE. Not in *that* outfit. (*To* NORA.) Unless it's come-as-you-are?

NORA. I believe Mister Flinder said informal.

WINIFRED. Good, then I'm all set.

BONNIE. Mother . . . !

WINIFRED. Oh, I'll change, I'll change. Can't you take a joke?

BONNIE. Not lately. (*To* NORA:) Who's coming, anyhow? Is it going to be a very *big* party—?

NORA. Only three besides the family and Miss Threadgill—Doctor Morgan, Mrs. Gullock, and that young Mister Metzel.

BONNIE. *Tony's* coming? Good heavens, I've got to change!

WINIFRED. But darling, you look charming.

BONNIE. When a woman cares for a man, she puts on her very best. (*Heads for stairs, on:*)

NORA. Miss Bonnie—I didn't know you cared for Tony Metzel.

BONNIE. Nora, I don't!

WINIFRED. Then why—?

BONNIE. I don't want *him* to know that! (*Exits up stairs.*)

NORA. (*Rushes to foot of stairs, calls up:*) Oh, and I forgot—that Doctor Lennimer is coming, too!

BONNIE. (*Off.*) Then you'd better hide the gladiolas! It's going to be enough of a wake as it is!

NORA. (*Heading back toward bowl on table.*) As if I didn't have enough to do already—!

WINIFRED. Now, now, Nora, don't go to too much trouble.

NORA. I've got to make some kind of hors d'oeuvres . . . (*Picks up bowl.*)

WINIFRED. Crackers and dip should be enough, if we're generous with the liquor.

NORA. (*Sees pamphlet on table.*) What's that?

WINIFRED. Just something Lorelei left for me to read. You'd better leave it out, so I can pretend I've been poring over its every word. It's an exercise book.

NORA. A nice romantic novel would do you more good. A woman in your condition needs a good cry.

WINIFRED. (*Holds kitchen door open for* NORA.) If I

do yoga exercises, I'll probably end up crying to beat the band. Did I ever tell you about the time Marian Harper got stuck in the lotus position . . . ? (NORA *exits with bowl,* WINIFRED *exits after her.*)

(*Even as the door is swinging shut behind them,* ADDISON *comes downstairs; he is in sportcoat and slacks, and his manner is furtive; he looks about to make sure he is alone, then goes to desk, picks up phone and dials.*)

ADDISON. (*On phone.*) . . . Hello—Lorelei? Addison . . . May I please speak with Tony? . . . Thank you . . . (*Darts anxious look toward kitchen and stairs while waiting; then:*) Tony? Addison . . . I'd like to ask you a question . . . Can you possibly psychoanalyze a person without their knowledge? . . . Why *not?* . . . Well, how do psychiatrists test people who *won't* cooperate? . . . But that's the very thing I want—give someone the once-over in a situation they don't know is clinical! . . . Yes, even an *indication* of a sorry mental state would be a big help—that is, it wouldn't make me *happy,* but I'd know where matters stood . . . With *Winifred,* of course! . . . That's just it—I don't *know!* The uncertainty is what's driving me crazy . . . No, I don't want you to psychoanalyze *me!* That was a figure of speech! . . . Yes? . . . Well, of *course* the rest of us will cooperate with your plan—what *is* your plan? . . . (*DOOR CHIMES sound.*) Oh, damn, there's the door—someone will be coming to answer it! You'd better fill me in when you get here— *Oh!* Listen—Ring one-one-three, so I'll know it's you at the door, got it? . . . Right! See you in a few minutes! (*Hangs up, exits swiftly through foyer.* WINIFRED *enters from kitchen, is almost to foyer when* ADDISON *enters with* PHILIP, *who is elegantly but casually garbed, also.*)
WINIFRED. Oh, you got the door, Addison! Good evening, Philip.

PHILIP. (*Eyeing her garb.*) Uh—good evening, Winifred. How casual *is* this gathering?

WINIFRED. Don't be ridiculous, Philip. I'm just going upstairs to change.

ADDISON. She dressed like that for dinner.

WINIFRED. Well, it wasn't *my* idea!

PHILIP. Oh, please don't change on *my* account, Winifred. (NORA *enters from kitchen with ice bucket, carries it to bar, during:*)

WINIFRED. Rest assured, Philip, rest assured! *I'm* dressing for *Lorelei's* sake! (*Exits up stairs.*)

PHILIP. If I thought I'd catch *Bonnie* in an outfit like that, I would have arrived unforgiveably *early!*

NORA. (*Politely.*) You *did.* (*Exits to kitchen.*)

ADDISON. You mustn't mind Nora. That's just her way. And you *are* a bit beforehand, you know.

PHILIP. I don't mind Nora making a joke—I just hate her topping one of *mine!*

ADDISON. (*Chuckles briefly, then sobers for:*) Actually, Philip, I'm glad you're early. I want to talk with you about Winifred before the others get here.

PHILIP. Now, Addison, I've already *told* you that with a small amount of indulgence on your part, she'll come out of it just fine . . .

ADDISON. I know what you told me, Philip. And believe me, I respect your good intentions.

PHILIP. (*On uncertain footing.*) You—you make that sound as if you didn't believe me . . .

ADDISON. I must confess—I found out the truth this afternoon. I know all about Winifred's *real* condition. (*Holds up a hand to forestall protest.*) Philip, there's no need to apologize. I understand why you had to make up that story. You were simply telling me that for my own good. I appreciate it.

PHILIP. (*Caught—he thinks—and thus relieved.*) I must say—I'm glad you know. Keeping up a deception is a lot harder than one thinks. Does Winifred know you know?

ADDISON. Good heavens, no! The least I can do is pretend I believe what you told me.

PHILIP. (*Takes check from pocket.*) Well, in that case, you may as well have this. I wasn't going to cash it. But if I'd refused your offer, you would have become suspicious.

ADDISON. (*Takes it, bewildered.*) But—this is the money to cover Winifred's hospitalization and care.

PHILIP. Under the circumstances, I can hardly accept it, Addison.

ADDISON. Oh, now, wait. Fair is fair. You did your best, Philip. Here, please take it back.

PHILIP. (*Thunderstruck.*) You're not serious? This is an awful lot of money, Addison.

ADDISON. I can afford it, Philip. Go on, take it.

PHILIP. (*Dazed but pleased, pockets check, on:*) Who says crime doesn't pay!

ADDISON. Really, Philip, I wish you wouldn't make *quite* so light of the matter!

PHILIP. (*At sea.*) Sorry . . . but, I mean, it's not every day I get such a windfall for doing absolutely nothing.

ADDISON. Nothing? You did perform the operation, didn't you?

PHILIP. (*Totally lost, and scared.*) Uh—you mean— the operation on Winifred—?

ADDISON. Well, I'd hardly pay you for operating on a stranger! Tell me, in all honesty— How long has my poor wife got? Bonnie said it was a matter of days, but I'd like to hear it from a medical authority.

PHILIP. (*In need of an ally.*) Say, where *is* Bonnie, anyhow? I'd like to talk to her . . .

ADDISON. Time enough for that, later. First, I'd like to hear the truth about Winifred. Will it happen gradually, or all at once?

PHILIP. (*Stalling while seeking a clue.*) Oh, these things —take time.

ADDISON. Yes, but how much time? She already thinks

she spent yesterday shopping in Paris! She said so, right in this room. Even *Bonnie* said she was nuts.

PHILIP. Well—now—Bonnie's bright enough, but the average layman can't recognize insanity in its subtler forms. Without special training, you can't tell paranoia from pyromania.

ADDISON. My thinking, exactly! That's why I've asked Tony Metzel here tonight. He assures me he can probe her mind without her even realizing what he's doing.

PHILIP. Addison, I don't understand— What's he probing *for?*

ADDISON. Much as I respect your opinion as a doctor, I need a specialist on mental disease.

PHILIP. I could use one, myself! . . . Just how does he plan to analyze her without her knowledge?

ADDISON. I didn't have time to ask him.

PHILIP. Don't you think you'd better? If he ties her to the sofa, she's going to suspect *something!*

ADDISON. By the way, there'll be another doctor along, tonight. Do you know our neighbor, Doctor Lennimer?

PHILIP. Can't say as I do. What's his field?

ADDISON. I'm not sure. Perhaps Miss Threadgill can tell you—she's over at his house right now.

PHILIP. What's she doing *there?*

ADDISON. Ah-ah! Mustn't be jealous. After all, Philip, you do rather ignore the poor girl.

PHILIP. Really, Addison! I only meant she should be here attending to Winifred. Doesn't your wife mind?

ADDISON. Oh, Winifred doesn't know he's a doctor. She thinks he's a piano teacher.

PHILIP. Why should she think a thing like that?

ADDISON. Who knows? Why does she think Miss Threadgill is a brownie?

PHILIP. Brownie? You mean—one of the wee folk? Sitting on a mushroom?

ADDISON. *Now* do you believe there's something wrong with my wife's mind?

PHILIP. Well—with hers or *yours*. I think I need a drink.

ADDISON. Oh, certainly. You know where it is. I'll see if Nora has the hors d'oeuvres ready. (ADDISON *exits to kitchen;* PHILIP *goes to bar, doesn't see what he wants, stoops out of sight behind it to search. At that moment,* MAXINE *and* WALDO *enter through patio, garbed as before.*)

MAXINE. Waldo, I've got to hurry up and change for the party. I'd ask you to have a drink while you're waiting, but it's not my house.

WALDO. Won't Doctor Morgan object to your changing? You're still here on duty, I mean. (PHILIP *rises, unnoticed by them, listening, just behind* MAXINE.)

MAXINE. I could arrive stark *naked* and *he* wouldn't notice!

WALDO. (*Fondly.*) *I* would.

MAXINE. (*Tenderly.*) That's the difference between you and Doctor Morgan. You're sensitive to people's needs. I'll bet it's a great help in your work.

WALDO. Oh, it is. I remember when Mrs. Miller first brought her boy to me. He had no feeling whatsoever, and— Well, just imagine going through *life* with no ear!

MAXINE. How terrible!

WALDO. It was a classic case—his coordination was ghastly, and he was totally lacking in color. But today, he plays like all the other children!

MAXINE. Oh, Waldo, I—I could cry! Next to you, Doctor Morgan is— (*Turns away, comes face to face with* PHILIP.)

WALDO. Is what?

MAXINE. (*Hopelessly.*) Next to *me*.

WALDO. Huh?

MAXINE. (*Bolts for stairs.*) I've got to go upstairs and change! (*Exits on:*)

PHILIP. (*Calls after her:*) *You'll* never change! (*To* WALDO, *conversationally:*) Some day I'm going to write her up for a medical journal: "My Four Years with An Albatross!" . . . I'm Philip Morgan.

WALDO. It figures. (*Shakes hands with* PHILIP, *reluctantly*.) I'm Waldo Lennimer. I live next door.

PHILIP. I was quite intrigued by what you were telling Miss Threadgill. The little boy without an ear—?

WALDO. (*Modestly*.) Oh, well, all in a day's work. I may have exaggerated a bit for Maxine's benefit.

PHILIP. Even so, I'm impressed. You must be quite skilled. I don't know what *I'd* do in a case like that. I mean, a kid with no ear—

WALDO. Oh, he had an ear, all right. I just helped him *find* it! (*As* PHILIP *reacts*, ADDISON *enters from kitchen, sees the two men, and hastens to join them*.)

ADDISON. Ah, I see you've met! I hope you haven't been making any plans. I want to hear Tony's, first.

WALDO. Who is Tony?

ADDISON. A sort of psychiatrist. I guess you wonder why I need one?

WALDO. Not really.

PHILIP. If the women are here when he arrives, how's he going to tell us his plan?

ADDISON. The moment he rings the bell, we'll send the women out on the terrace, or something.

WALDO. How will you know it's Tony ringing?

ADDISON. We have a prearranged signal.

PHILIP. Would you care to let us in on it? I do my best work in prepared cahoots. (*DOOR CHIMES sound; chimes are the two-note kind, and we hear them once . . . once again . . . then three times in fast succession*.)

ADDISON. Ah! Do you know what *that* is?

WALDO. (*Nods*.) "Sentimental Journey."

PHILIP. (*With genuine admiration*.) By golly, you're right!

ADDISON. (*Irked by their lack of concern*.) Oh, for heaven's sake! (NORA *comes from kitchen to answer door; he instantly waves her back*.) Never mind, Nora.

I'll let Tony in— Whoever it is. (NORA *shrugs and exits to kitchen.*) I hope she didn't hear what I said.

PHILIP. If she didn't, she'll answer the door. (*DOOR CHIMES sound the one-one-three again.*)

ADDISON. (*Starts for foyer.*) Now, remember, gentlemen—not a word to the women! (*Exits.*)

WALDO. It's going to be a very quiet evening . . . Unless *you* know what he's talking about?

PHILIP. I thought I did when I got here, but I lost the thread someplace.

WALDO. I know what you mean. When Maxine and I started to tell him about all that transplanting this morning, he shouted something about ladies being present.

PHILIP. Transplant? And Maxine assisted you?

WALDO. She was very helpful. I just held out my hand and she slapped the right tool into it.

PHILIP. But, damn it all—she's supposed to be on duty *here!*

WALDO. Oh, Mrs. Flinder said she could. After all, it was an emergency, and it's only just next door.

PHILIP. Where? You mean here, in Tarrytown? I should think you'd go to a hospital!

WALDO. What for? My garden's just down the driveway.

PHILIP. Hold on—just exactly what sort of transplant did you do?

WALDO. We won't know that till judgment day. Maxine promised to be there.

PHILIP. She gets a choice?!

(ADDISON *scurries in, followed by* TONY METZEL—*a lad who looks excessively callow when he's not acting knowledgeable; he is in his mid-twenties and reasonably attractive.* LORELEI *enters at a slower pace, in a rather elegant cocktail dress, but still toting the gargantuan purse.*)

ADDISON. Tony, I'd like you to meet Waldo Lennimer. You know Philip, of course.

TONY. How do you do, sir. It's an honor. (*Shakes* WALDO'S *hand.*) I understand you practice next door.

WALDO. Have the Swensons been complaining again? (*To* PHILIP.) I stop cold at ten o'clock every night. You know how neighbors are.

LORELEI. Ah, Doctor Lennimer! I hope you're over your little upset? Winifred told me on the telephone this afternoon. I understand Miss Threadgill gave you every assistance in repairing the damage.

WALDO. She was magnificent. Steady hands and a wonderful sense of balance. I'd never have put things in the proper place without her.

ADDISON. (*Eager to halt the chitchat.*) Winifred's upstairs dressing. Perhaps you'd like to join her?

LORELEI. Why, yes, I would! Point me the way. I hope I'm in time to see her scar!

ADDISON. (*Escorting her to stairs.*) First door on your left at the top. (*As* LORELEI *ascends, he watches till she is out of earshot, during:*)

PHILIP. Waldo—what do your neighbors have to do with your practice?

WALDO. As little as possible. They say they can't stand the noise. I still make a lot of mistakes. Sometimes I sing loud to cover up. (*As* PHILIP *reacts,* ADDISON *hurries to join the group, on:*)

ADDISON. Quickly, Tony—what's your plan?!

TONY. When the women come down, we play a little game . . .

PHILIP. What kind of game, Tony?

TONY. We send Winifred out of the room, and we tell her when she gets back, she has to guess the plot of a story we made up while she was gone.

WALDO. That doesn't sound like much fun.

ADDISON. It's not supposed to be fun!

WALDO. What kind of party *is* this?

ADDISON. Philip, didn't you tell him?

PHILIP. Tell him what? I haven't heard Tony's plan yet.

ADDISON. (*To* WALDO.) Tony's a psychiatrist.

PHILIP. Not quite.

ADDISON. That's beside the point!

WALDO. *What* point?

TONY. Will you let me finish?!

ADDISON. Of course, my boy, of course. Go on!

TONY. Actually, we don't make up a story at all. Then, when she comes back in the room—

WALDO. We yell "April Fool"?

ADDISON. Of course we don't—! (*To* TONY, *less certainly.*) Do we?

TONY. Look, I'll explain to everybody when Winifred's out of the room!

PHILIP. She *is* out of the room!

WALDO. She's not missing much.

ADDISON. Doctor Lennimer, this is a serious matter! Philip, haven't you told him *anything?*

PHILIP. Well—we got to talking about ears . . .

ADDISON. At a time like this?!

WALDO. A time like *what!?*

ADDISON. Doctor, my wife is on the threshhold of madness . . . !

TONY. And it's my job to pull her through!

PHILIP. How do you mean that?

TONY. Doctor Lennimer—do you know anything about paranoia?

WALDO. I had a friend once who was paranoiac. He was terrified of everything. He was even afraid to answer the telephone. Then he went to see an analyst. He was in therapy for a whole year.

ADDISON. How did he come out of it?

WALDO. Oh, fine—just fine. Now he answers the telephone whether it rings or not.

ADDISON. Doctor Lennimer—!

PHILIP. Tony, we're not even *discussing* paranoia! What Winifred has is quite common to women who've had such an operation. It is a slight touch of cyclothymia, that's all.

TONY. Ah, but doesn't cyclothymia often turn into melancholia?

PHILIP. Well, sometimes, but—

TONY. And melancholia almost inevitably becomes manic-depressive insanity, doesn't it?

ADDISON. Oh, my poor darling!

WALDO. Excuse me, but if anybody is nuts around here, I think it's the three of you! So she's got cyclo-whatever-it-is! Doctor Morgan says it's natural after her operation. You're all trying to parlay a skinned knee into a severed artery!

PHILIP. He's got a point, Addison. I'm sure Winifred's condition is just a temporary one. It will pass, in time.

TONY. Into melancholia!

WALDO. (*Picks up pamphlet.*) Whose is this?

ADDISON. (*Distracted, glances at pamphlet.*) Oh, that's just something Lorelei Gullock left for my wife to read, this morning. Or at least, I think it is.

PHILIP. Seems to me when I was on the telephone, she said something about a woman on her knees—? (*Moves up to look closer at pamphlet.*)

WALDO. Then this is the one, all right! . . . Tony, I apologize.

ADDISON. Why? What is it? Let me see!

PHILIP. (*Who has seen, tries to forestall* ADDISON.) Now—maybe she just being polite to Lorelei—

ADDISON. (*Grabs pamphlet from* WALDO, *looks.*) This is a *recruiting* pamphlet from the *Carmelite Nuns!*

TONY. Oh, I'm *so* glad she's looking on the bright side!

ADDISON. *I* don't want my wife entering a *convent!*

WALDO. It sure beats a padded cell.

PHILIP. I'm sure there's been some mistake. Winifred wouldn't *contemplate*—I mean, *do* such a thing.

ADDISON. You *said* she might feel she was no longer a *woman*—!

WALDO. In *that* case, she'd join the *Trappists!*

TONY. Look, speculation will get us nowhere. When

she comes down, Mister Flinder, why don't you simply *ask* her?

PHILIP. Of course! The direct approach is always the simplest and best.

ADDISON. You're right, of course. I should have thought of that, myself. I don't know what it is—ever since we arrived here, today, things have been so damned discomfitting—!

WALDO. It's the brownies. (*Others look at him.*) Don't stare like that. I know it sounds stupid, but that's only because you haven't lived in Tarrytown as long as I have. Would you believe this house used to be a meeting-place for them?

ADDISON. Doctor Lennimer—what in the world are you talking about?

WALDO. Brownies. Little people. The good folk. The lady who used to live here simply doted on them. If you're smart, so will you.

PHILIP. I'm afraid I don't follow you.

TONY. *I'm* afraid I *do* follow him!

WALDO. Look, it's no big deal, it's just a fact of life in this neighborhood. I didn't leave a saucer of milk out for them last night, because it was raining. This morning, Bonnie Flinder cut down my prize gladiolas.

TONY. Addison, are you sure I'm here to analyze *Winifred—?*

WALDO. Okay, okay! *Don't* believe me. But be honest with yourself, Mister Flinder— Haven't you sensed the *wrongness* of the place? Since you got here today, haven't you noticed the atmosphere of mischief and dizzy confusion in your home?

ADDISON. Now that you mention it— But this is ridiculous! *Brownies?*

WALDO. I tried to tell your wife and daughter this morning, but—

PHILIP. Addison, that's *it!* Winifred isn't having aberrations—she's just quoting her nutty neighbor!

ADDISON. But what about the trip to Paris? And why

did *Bonnie* say her mother was nuts? (*As others ponder this:*) Look, what we need is a good stiff drink. Come on, men. (*All go upstage to bar.*)

PHILIP. You got any Metaxa?

ADDISON. (*En route behind bar.*) How about Metaxa Manhattans? They should put us back in a party mood.

PHILIP. Great! Make mine on the rocks. How about you men? (*Others ad-lib assent, then* PHILIP, TONY *and* WALDO *sit on stools Left of bar, as* PHILIP *continues, to* TONY:) I'm afraid I haven't kept up to date on modern psychiatry. Just how does this game work?

TONY. Well, basically, it's designed so that the person asking the questions is actually creating her *own* story. As we listen to the story, we can see how her mind works, so we know where we're at.

WALDO. And where is that?

ADDISON. (*Mixing drinks.*) Really, Doctor Lennimer, it should be obvious! The story reflects the type of mentality that produced it. Right, Tony?

TONY. Right. If it's a normal story, we know the person is normal—

PHILIP. If it's a nutty story, we know the person is a nut.

WALDO. What if it's a cowboy story?

ADDISON. Will you be serious?!

WALDO. I'm very serious. I don't see how a party game can—

ADDISON. Quiet! I hear them coming! (WINIFRED *and* BONNIE, *in attractive cocktail dresses, descend the stairs with* LORELEI *and cross to Center, on:*)

PHILIP. Quick, let's talk about something else! Waldo, tell them about the little boy with no ear.

TONY. You think he ought to tell that one in mixed company?

PHILIP. I don't see what's wrong with it . . . ?

TONY. Is it the one that ends, "Never mind the grizzly bear—what did you do with the rhubarb!"?

ADDISON. I haven't heard that one. Why don't you tell it?

TONY. But now you all know the punch-line!

WALDO. I'd *still* like to hear what leads up to it!

PHILIP. So would I!

TONY. (*After glance toward women, lowers voice for:*) Well— There's this kid with only one ear, see? And he decides to go to Tibet and ask the Grand Lama how come he's been doomed to go through life with his . . . (TONY'S *voice fades out as he and others at bar go into a huddle so the women can't hear; during the following,* ADDISON—*always keeping an ear turned to* TONY— *finishes preparing the drinks, and passes them to each man.*)

LORELEI. Let's not interrupt them. I hear Tony plans to organize some kind of game, tonight. I hate party games.

WINIFRED. Well, Lorelei, there's only so much gossip. And I don't think the men would be interested in hearing it.

BONNIE. Don't count on that. Remember, I've been in on every one of our company's inventors' councils.

WINIFRED. You *said* they didn't *count* as men!

LORELEI. (*Sets her purse on table.*) I don't really mind games—it's just the ones that require a lot of spelling. And tonight—well, with Doctor Morgan, Doctor Lennimer, and Tony—! Who invented medical terminology, anyhow?

BONNIE. Well, now, you can't count Doctor Lennimer, Mrs. Gullock.

LORELEI. Musicians are even worse! Could you stake your life on the proper spelling of *"andante cantabile"?* (*Squints at pamphlet.*) Oh, I see you've been reading this thing. Or have you?

WINIFRED. Every word. It's most interesting.

BONNIE. Mother intends to put it into practice at the first opportunity.

LORELEI. Good, good. There's nothing like yoga for

filling your body with serenity, self-control and a deep
and lasting inner peace.

WINIFRED. What about a hormone shortage?

LORELEI. What do you want—egg in your beer?! (*At
bar, men abruptly explode outward from each other in
a chorus of roaring laughter, distracting women, who look
Upstage curiously.*)

PHILIP. (*Wheezing with delight.*) ". . . what did you
do with the *rhubarb?*"!

WALDO. You know, I think it's funnier when you *know*
what the punch-line is!

ADDISON. (*With jocular approval.*) Tony, you ought to
be ashamed of yourself!

TONY. *I* didn't make it up! I just tells 'em as I hears
'em!

BONNIE. Hey, that must have been a beaut. Let *us* in
on it!

ADDISON. (*Instantly somber, coming out from behind
bar.*) You wouldn't get it.

PHILIP. (*Still wheezing with mirth, elbows* ADDISON
amicably in the ribs.) You mean you *hope* she wouldn't!

BONNIE. Mother, will you promise to pry it out of Dad
later? I *hate* floating punch-lines!

ADDISON. Bonnie, I wouldn't tell your mother a story
like that!

LORELEI. Don't worry, dear. *I'll* tell it to you.

WALDO. *You* know that joke?

TONY. Where do you think *I* heard it?!

LORELEI. (*To* WOMEN.) And *I* only told him the *polite*
version! (*All laugh; then, as* BONNIE *starts blithely
toward bar,* TONY *comes down and starts to separate the
two sofa-segments so that they now slightly face one
another from Upper Right and Upper Left of the table,
with about a four-foot gap between their Upstage ends.*)

BONNIE. Why don't I whip up something for the ladies
—as long as chivalry is dead?! (MAXINE *descends stairs
into room, dressed in a truly lovely, and singularly inap-
propriate, floor-length Japanese kimono, during:*)

ADDISON. I mixed a double batch, dear. There's plenty in the pitcher. (BONNIE *pours drinks for ladies, including one for* MAXINE, *during:*)

LORELEI. Tony, what in the world are you doing?

TONY. Just setting up for a little game, Aunt Lorelei.

MAXINE. Is it charades? I love charades!

PHILIP. (*Noticing her for first time.*) Well! If it isn't Nurse Butterfly! You see, you were wrong: I *did* notice you.

WALDO. It doesn't count. She's not naked.

(*Over next dozen lines, group gets settled into place for what will be "game positions";* BONNIE *will give individual drinks to the other women before they take seats, and bring her own down to the game area, at the same time; when all are seated—with* TONY *Downstage of Left sofa segment on chair which he takes from position near Downstage Left wall, arrangement of persons at the start of game will be:*

WINIFRED		PHILIP
ADDISON		LORELEI
WALDO	TABLE	MAXINE
BONNIE		TONY

The foursome on Right sofa will be crowded at first, but BONNIE, WALDO *and* ADDISON *can spread out once* WINIFRED *gets up.*)

PHILIP. By the way, Miss Threadgill, I understand you were demonstrating your expertise with Waldo earlier today. I didn't know you could assist at a transplant.

WINIFRED. You probably didn't know she was a Brownie.

ADDISON. Now, Winifred—!

WINIFRED. (*Squirming.*) Addison, can't you shift down a bit? I'm ready to go over the edge!

ADDISON. Nonsense! You're perfectly normal!

TONY. (*Interrupting deftly.*) Don't worry, Mrs. Flinder. You can be the first one out of the room!

MAXINE. Oh, let *me!*

PHILIP. Really, Miss Threadgill, as long as Winifred is our hostess, we should let her go first.

WINIFRED. No, let Maxine go. I don't mind.

ADDISON. Well, I do! You're going first, Winifred, and that's all there is to it!

BONNIE. Dad, you mustn't excite yourself! It's bad for your blood pressure.

PHILIP. Bonnie's right, Addison. I'm sure Winifred won't mind going first.

WINIFRED. (*Rises resignedly.*) Oh, all right. Anything to keep Addison's voice down! (*To* TONY:) I'll be out on the patio if you need me. (*Turns and exits onto patio, remaining in view, but all the way Upstage to the low stone wall, her back toward the room.*)

TONY. (*Waits till she is as far as she's going, then hunches forward conspiratorially.*) Now, listen carefully, everybody. When she comes back, I'll tell her we all concocted a story in her absence, and that it's her job to ferret the story out of us by questioning . . .

MAXINE. Oh, that's fun! Let me start first: "Once upon a time—"

TONY. Wait! We don't actually concoct a story at all! We just tell *her* that.

BONNIE. But, Tony—how can we possibly answer her questions, if—?

TONY. I'm *coming* to that!

WINIFRED. (*Turns head slightly.*) Ready or not, here I come—!

ADDISON. No! Not yet!

WINIFRED. Well, hurry it up! It's getting chilly out here!

TONY. We're almost ready! Just another minute! (*To group:*) Here's what we do: When she starts the questioning, if her question ends in a vowel, whoever she asks answers *yes.* If it ends in a consonant, you answer *no.* But if it ends in a *y,* you answer, "In a way." Got it, now? Any questions?

BONNIE. I'm not sure I understand the *point* of the game—

TONY. The whole idea is—*she's* the one who actually makes up the story. It's—um—it's sort of a *fun*-form of psychoanalysis . . .

BONNIE. Oh, now, wait just a minute! I'm not going to let my mother—

ADDISON. Bonnie, don't interfere! Your mother needs help!

BONNIE. Well, of all the silly, childish—! Dad, are you going to let this beardless boy—!?

WINIFRED. What's going on in there? Am I missing a fight?

TONY. Only a few more seconds, Mrs. Flinder! (*To group:*) Everybody understand what to do?

MAXINE. I don't understand one part of it—what's a consonant?

WALDO. Anything that isn't a vowel— (*Sees her blank stare, reminds her gallantly:*) A-E-I-O-U . . . ?

LORELEI. Tony, I forget—which is yes and which is no . . . ?

TONY. (*With ill-controlled exasperation:*) Vowel—yes! Consonant—no! The letter *y*—"In a way!" Okay?

WINIFRED. Can I come in, now?

MAXINE. *NO!* (*To* TONY, *brightly:*) Did I do it right?

TONY. (*Stops short of a sharp answer, and just nods, smiling wanly.*) Just perfectly. Now, let's get on with it. (*Calls:*) All right, Mrs. Flinder! You can come in, now!

WINIFRED. (*Enters from patio.*) What's the object of the game—chilblains or pneumonia? (*Stops at space between upper ends of sofas, remains standing, takes a sip of her drink on:*)

MAXINE. (*In deep distress.*) Waldo—I don't know how to spell pneumonia!

BONNIE. Maybe we *should* have sent Maxine out first!

ADDISON. Bonnie—!

BONNIE. But think of the wonderful story we're missing!

WINIFRED. What—?

TONY. (*Quickly.*) Let me tell you what's up, Mrs. Flinder. While you were gone, we all collaborated on a story, and what you have to do is guess the story by asking us questions.

WINIFRED. What's the plot?

TONY. Wait— The questions have to be phrased so that we can answer only yes or no or "In a way!"

WINIFRED. What's "In a Way!"?

TONY. Oh—you know—if your question is partly right, but not quite.

WINIFRED. Oh, yes, I see. All right. Where do I start?

TONY. Anywhere you want.

WINIFRED. (*Surveys group carefully, considering; then:*) Okay. I know who I'm going to start with. Maxine?

MAXINE. The answer is yes!

WINIFRED. Yes *what?*

MAXINE. The answer is no!

PHILIP. Maxine Threadgill, are you crazy?!

MAXINE. In a way!

BONNIE. Say, you know, Tony—I *like* this game!

(TONY *jumps up, wordlessly takes* MAXINE *by the arm, and pulls her out onto the patio; others all look that direction, and we hear* TONY *and* MAXINE, *in "whispery"—but loud—voices, babbling at one another* simultaneously:)

MAXINE. . . . tried to play right . . . everything she asked . . . got all the consonants and vowels . . . did the best I could . . .	TONY. . . . how stupid can one girl possibly get! . . . don't answer *normal* questions by the rules . . . where are your brains? . . . can't you get *anything* right! . . .

(*Then, separately:*)

MAXINE. I'm *sorry!* I'm sorry!

TONY. (*Quivering with rage.*) Okay. Okay. One more chance! (*They return to their places in the group, while others try to look as if nothing unusual had occurred; then, after all slightly sigh with relief:*)

WINIFRED. (*Still standing, goes on brightly:*) Maybe if I use the animal-mineral-vegetable approach—?

ADDISON. Splendid idea, darling! That sounds quite sound!

WALDO. I beg your pardon?

TONY. (*Through gritted teeth.*) Shut up!

WINIFRED. (*Hastening to restore peace.*) Let me start with Bonnie . . . Does the story have anything to do with animal life?

BONNIE. (*Hesitates; gets furious glower from* TONY, *gives in and says flatly:*) . . . Yes.

WINIFRED. (*To* WALDO:) Is it a domestic animal?

WALDO. (*Pauses to figure final letter; then:*) No.

WINIFRED. Hmm . . . Some sort of wild animal, then . . . (*Looks about, notes moosehead on wall, turns brightly to* ADDISON, *and:*) Does it have something to do with the moose—?

ADDISON. Uh . . . Oh! Yes! Yes, it does!

WINIFRED. (*To* PHILIP:) Is it who the moose looks like?

PHILIP. (*Baffled, but following the rules.*) Why— Yes!

WINIFRED. (*Incredulously, to* ADDISON:) The story's about your *mother?!*

ADDISON. *NO!*

BONNIE. Well, he's sticking to the rules . . . !

TONY. Bonnie, *please!*

WINIFRED. (*To* ADDISON:) Then *whose* mother—*mine?*

ADDISON. (*Helpless under the rules.*) Um—oh—well— *yes*, damn it!

WINIFRED. You think my mother looks like that moose?!

ADDISON. (*Looks at* TONY, *then says miserably:*) Yes! (MAXINE *giggles;* WINIFRED *whirls on her.*)

WINIFRED. I suppose you think that's funny?

MAXINE. (*Wide-eyed, but loyal to the game.*) . . . In a way!

WINIFRED. Addison, aren't you ashamed of yourself?!

ADDISON. (*Sinking rapidly into despair.*) . . . *NO!*

BONNIE. (*Doubling over with laughter.*) Tony, this is a *scream . . . !*

ADDISON. Bonnie, will you for heaven's sake be serious!?

WINIFRED. During a party game?

MAXINE. (*Getting the hang of it.*) *YES!*

WINIFRED. I beg your pardon?

MAXINE. *NO!*

WALDO. (*To* ADDISON, *quietly:*) *Now* do you believe in brownies? (GUNTHER *enters from patio.*)

GUNTHER. I think the putting green is finished.

ADDISON. Don't you know?

GUNTHER. It's pretty dark out back.

LORELEI. Your own putting green, Addison? I'd like to see it!

GUNTHER. You may have to wait till daylight.

LORELEI. (*Takes huge flashlight from purse.*) That's what you think. (*Starts for patio.*)

TONY. Wait a minute—what about the game?

WINIFRED. Yes, I haven't guessed the story yet.

ADDISON. It was a stupid story, anyhow!

MAXINE. Oh, good! Can *I* go out next?

TONY. By all means, go!

PHILIP. But Tony— (*Looks after departing* MAXINE.) A person who knows the *rules* can't go out . . . ?

TONY. What makes you think I'm going to call her *back!?*

WALDO. Well, of all the dirty tricks—! (*Starts after her.*) Maxine! Maxine, wait for me! (*As* LORELEI, MAXINE *and* WALDO *vanish,* PHILIP *gets to his feet.*)

PHILIP. Guess I may as well join the group, while Lorelei's batteries last.

BONNIE. (*Joins him, takes his arm.*) Mind if I tag along? I'd like to have a little talk with you . . .

PHILIP. (*Flattered.*) You'd like my opinion on something?

BONNIE. Actually, I'd like your *endorsement!* (PHILIP *reacts unhappily, but goes out with her, as:*)

ADDISON. What in the world does Bonnie mean?

WINIFRED. I haven't the vaguest notion, dear. (*Shouts after* BONNIE:) If you haven't got a pen, check with Lorelei! (*Turns back, forestalls* ADDISON's *forthcoming question with:*) Just making small talk.

GUNTHER. Shall I clear up this mess before I go? (*Indicates glasses on table.*)

ADDISON. I wish you could! . . . Oh, *that* stuff! Yes, by all means. (GUNTHER *clears glasses, first stuffing pamphlet in pocket, exits to kitchen during:*)

TONY. You shouldn't have let them interrupt the game, Mister Flinder.

WINIFRED. You make it sound so important . . . ?

ADDISON. Never mind the silly game. I'm tired of being devious. The best approach is a direct one.

WINIFRED. The best approach to what?

ADDISON. (*Points at bare table with looking.*) What exactly is the meaning of that?! (*Following his indication, blinks.*) Where did it go?

TONY. Mister Chowdy must have picked it up. Shall I—? (*Takes halfstep toward kitchen.*)

ADDISON. Yes—no—wait. Look, never mind about that, but—would you leave us alone for a few minutes, Tony?

TONY. Oh, certainly. I understand. (*Exits to kitchen.*)

WINIFRED. *I* don't. Addison, what is going on here?

ADDISON. I'd like to know the meaning of that pamphlet Lorelei left you!

WINIFRED. Did you read it?

ADDISON. All I cared to!

WINIFRED. Then what's to tell? Lorelei thought it would be just the thing for a woman in my condition.

ADDISON. How dare she even suggest such a thing?!

WINIFRED. What are you so upset about? I could try it for awhile, and then if I didn't enjoy it, I could always quit.

ADDISON. Don't oversimplify, Winifred. It's not all that easy to get into, and even if you did, look at the position it would put me in!

WINIFRED. Put *you* in?!

ADDISON. Why are you even considering it? What would our friends say?

WINIFRED. But Addison, it's the *in*-thing to do. Even Marian Harper recommends it.

ADDISON. Why "even" Marian Harper?

WINIFRED. Oh, that's right, you didn't know. She tried it once, and couldn't get out again. (*Laughs.*) Can't you just picture her?!

ADDISON. I fail to see the humor, Winifred! You're my wife, and my wife you're going to stay!

WINIFRED. Was there ever a doubt? Addison, maybe you'd better sit down . . .

ADDISON. (*Sits instantly on sofa.*) Why? What are you going to tell me?

WINIFRED. Darling, you're so tense! It's not good for your ulcer.

ADDISON. And I suppose this little departure you plan *is?*

WINIFRED. I think it would be a *nice* change in my daily routine. And Lorelei says that if I go at it religiously—

ADDISON. Winifred Flinder, sit down! (*Startled,* WINIFRED *sits opposite* ADDISON *on other sofa.*)

WINIFRED. Addison, your blood pressure—!

ADDISON. Forget about me! Listen—darling—I know I'm supposed to humor you—

WINIFRED. You are?

ADDISON. It was Doctor Morgan's idea.

WINIFRED. I *told* you I didn't like Doctor Morgan!

ADDISON. At the moment, neither do I! Darling, I can't let you take this step!

WINIFRED. But whyever *not*, darling?

ADDISON. Well, for one thing, you're not a Catholic!

WINIFRED. You mean a Buddhist.

ADDISON. Do they let Buddhists join the Carmelites?!

WINIFRED. (*Rises.*) How the dickens should *I* know?! (*Starts for bar.*) While you make up your mind what we're talking about, I am going to have a good stiff drink!

ADDISON. (*Stands up, near to tears.*) Winifred, we've got to face the issue squarely! I am worried sick about your sanity!

WINIFRED. Well, I'm not exactly turning handsprings over *yours!* (*Rummages among bottles behind bar.*) Where the devil is that brandy?!

ADDISON. Aren't you befuddled enough already?!

WINIFRED. *Me?!* You haven't made a stick of sense since sundown! (*Finds brandy, pours a stiff shot.*)

ADDISON. If it's not asking too much, let's be logical about this. Were you or were you not in Paris yesterday?

WINIFRED. I—I wasn't, of course.

ADDISON. But didn't you say you were?

WINIFRED. Well . . . Yes, I did, but—

ADDISON. Why did you *say* it if is wasn't *true?!*

WINIFRED. (*Takes swallow of brandy; then:*) I—I guess I just wasn't myself . . .

ADDISON. Aha! Then you *admit* you've got problems!

WINIFRED. Everybody's got problems!

ADDISON. Everybody doesn't say Miss Threadgill is a brownie!

WINIFRED. What makes you think she's a Brownie?

ADDISON. You said she was!

WINIFRED. Well—she *was!*

ADDISON. And what is she right now?

WINIFRED. Well, I *hope* she's a *nurse!*

ADDISON. You're not sure?

WINIFRED. Not after listening to her!

ADDISON. Do you deny you said Doctor Lennimer was a piano teacher?

WINIFRED. Is there some reason I should? He *is* **a** piano teacher! Didn't he *say* he was a piano teacher?

ADDISON. I *made* him say that! But it's not true!

WINIFRED. Then why did you make him say it?

ADDISON. (*Finding the shoe is unaccountably on the wrong foot, sanity-wise:*) Because he—because you—well, under the circumstances—?! (*Realizes he is babbling; stops and takes a deep breath, then points an accusing finger at* WINIFRED, *on:*) Never mind all that! What *I* want to know is, how do you expect to solve your problems in a convent?!

WINIFRED. (*About to drink, chokes.*) Who said anything about a convent?!

ADDISON. (*Gives incoherent whimper; then:*) I've got to take a walk in the fresh air. My head is spinning! (*Starts toward patio.*)

WINIFRED. You're not dressed warmly enough! (*Turns away.*)

ADDISON. (*A groan of impotent rage.*) *I'll bundle up!* (*He turns up his jacket collar, tugs the entire thing up so that it completely conceals his head, and stalks furiously onto the patio and walks right by* MAXINE, *just coming in alone; she crosses the threshhold, then stops dead, a look of horror on her face, and as he vanishes from view:*)

MAXINE. (*Right out front.*) *Aaaaaaaaah!* The Headless Horseman! (WINIFRED *reacts, whirls to find source of scream;* TONY, GUNTHER *and* NORA *rush in from kitchen;* MAXINE *sways, places back of hand to forehead, and faints into the combined grasps of* GUNTHER *and* TONY; *they hastily carry her down and lay her on Left sofa-half, during:*)

NORA. The Headless Horseman? Where?!

TONY. Get her to the sofa, quick!

GUNTHER. Who's got some brandy?

WINIFRED. Here, she can take mine! (*As* GUNTHER *takes glass,* WALDO *comes rushing in from patio.*)

WALDO. I heard a scream! Who—? Maxine! What's happened?!

NORA. The poor dear saw the Headless Horseman!

TONY. Don't be ridiculous, Nora! This is the twentieth century!

WALDO. So maybe he was driving a *Mustang!* (*Rubbing* MAXINE's *wrists.*) Darling, are you all right?! (PHILIP, LORELEI *and* BONNIE *come rushing in through patio doors.*)

PHILIP. Here, now, what's going on?

LORELEI. Did she see it? Is that what it is?

WALDO. (*Jumps up, making room for* PHILIP *to take over wrist-chafing chore.*) Did *you* see something, Mrs. Gullock?

BONNIE. We both did! Just going around the side of the house. It was terribly dark, but I could see there was no head!

LORELEI. There wasn't even a *horse!*

NORA. Oh, glory be! Let's get out of this crazy town, Mrs. Flinder!

TONY. You're all talking nonsense! I'm sure there's a simple explanation.

BONNIE. Such as?

LORELEI. I know what I saw, Tony! He was about seven feet tall—

BONNIE. Well, he *would* have been, if he wasn't headless!

MAXINE. (*Stirs, abruptly sits up.*) Is he gone?!

PHILIP. You're supposed to say, "Where am I?"!

WALDO. Leave her alone! . . . Maxine, you go ahead and regain consciousness any way you want to!

BONNIE. This I've got to see!

MAXINE. But I *am* conscious!

NORA. Oh, Mrs. Flinder, let's go! Let's pack our bags and get out of this place!

WINIFRED. There *is* something strange about this house. I've just had the weirdest conversation with Addison—

BONNIE. Say, where *is* Dad?

NORA. The Horseman's taken him! I just know it! (GUNTHER *drinks brandy.*)

MAXINE. I never should have come to this crazy place! (*Offstage Left, there is a sudden hollow metallic* CLUNK, *followed by a yowl of anguish from* ADDISON, *followed by a ringing* CLANG.)

BONNIE. That was Dad!

WINIFRED. Oh, dear heaven!

NORA. (*Fleeing kitchenward.*) We'll all be murdered in our beds! Murdered in our beds! (*As she exits:*)

WINIFRED. Nora, one place is as good as another! (*Rushes toward foyer, preceded by all but* BONNIE *and* PHILIP.)

BONNIE. (*As all exit, turns to* PHILIP, *and:*) All right, Philip, this is your last chance. Are you going to give me that check or not?!

PHILIP. (*Smiles suavely.*) I think . . . *not.*

BONNIE. But you have no *right* to that money—!

PHILIP. Oh? For services rendered to your poor mother? And why not?

BONNIE. Because—because there *was* no operation, no hospital, no—

PHILIP. (*Interrupts deftly.*) So *you* say.

BONNIE. Listen, Philip, my mother *told* me about her trip to Paris—

PHILIP. And you believed her?

BONNIE. (*For the first time uneasy.*) Why— Philip, of *course* I— What are you implying?

PHILIP. Has it ever occurred to you that perhaps your mother *did* have that operation she denies?

BONNIE. (*It apparently has, but:*) . . . Mother wouldn't lie to me about a thing like that . . . !

PHILIP. Bonnie, my dear, a person who is mentally deranged is *incapable* of what *we* call a *lie.* Let's say she —simply doesn't recall.

BONNIE. Are you trying to tell me that Mother *is* nuts? Because if you *are—!*

PHILIP. I love the way your eyes flash when you're enraged.

BONNIE. Philip, you ain't seen *nothing* yet! If you expect me to believe—

PHILIP. You're no longer certain, are you!

BONNIE. Wh-why, of *course* I'm certain. M-mother simply . . . simply . . .

PHILIP. Pretended to go to the hospital? Then pretended to your father that she *had* gone? Pretended to be ill and nervous when she arrived here? Or did she pretend that she actually went to Paris?

BONNIE. (*No longer certain.*) But—you don't mean that her mind is really—Philip, if you're trying to scare me— (*She stops with a gasp as* GUNTHER *and* MAXINE *enter from foyer, carrying* ADDISON *by shoulders and ankles; he is clutching his head and moaning, while an anxious* WINIFRED *hovers at his side; a dazed* TONY *follows them, holding the horseshoe in his hands, his face horrified.*)

MAXINE. (*As she and* GUNTHER *set* ADDISON *upon the sofas which* WINIFRED *and* PHILIP *hastily rejoin:*) Where's Waldo? Where's my Waldo?

WINIFRED. He's putting Lorelei into Tony's car. She got pretty hysterical.

TONY. The Horseman . . . There *is* a Headless Horseman . . . There *must* be a—

BONNIE. Tony, don't *you* turn hysterical on us, too! You mustn't jump to conclusions about—

TONY. (*Brandishes horseshoe.*) Then where did *this* come from? Tell me that!

GUNTHER. A hardware store in Valhalla.

ADDISON. (*Sits up, woozily.*) Oh, my head! What happened? Did anyone get the license number?

WINIFRED. Now, now, darling, you just had a little accident.

BONNIE. There's hardly a bruise, Dad . . .

PHILIP. It seems minor enough, all right. Addison, you're going to be just fine!

ADDISON. Are you crazy? I've just been assaulted on my own front porch! What kind of a doctor are you, anyhow!? Give me back that check!

PHILIP. (*Starts to reach for it, then stops.*) I—I can't do that. It's gone!

MAXINE. The Horseman took it! I just know he did!

WINIFRED. Oh, come, now, Maxine! What would the Headless Horseman want that money for?

GUNTHER. Oats?

ADDISON. Philip, don't tell me you've *lost* it?

TONY. It's the brownies! They took it! We didn't leave them any milk and now we're paying for it!

ADDISON. If they took that check, *I'm* paying for it!

WALDO. (*Enters from foyer, on.*) Tony, your aunt wants you to take her home right away—

TONY. (*Hands* WALDO *horseshoe.*) Gladly! Anything to get out of this madhouse! Everybody's gone out of their minds! I'm not going to hang around crazy people! (*Exits through foyer.*)

BONNIE. Some psychiatrist!

ADDISON. Philip, what has become of that check?!

PHILIP. (*Flings up hands in surrender.*) Maxine's right. The Horseman took it!

ADDISON. (*Lurches to his feet.*) He's crazy, *too!* (*Staggers toward stairs, on:*) Good grief, it must be *contagious!* (*Starts up.*)

PHILIP. (*Can stand no more, heads for foyer.*) Winifred, I can't tell you how much I've enjoyed this evening!

MAXINE. (*As* PHILIP *exits.*) Why not?!

BONNIE. (*Heads for kitchen.*) I'd better see to Nora . . .

WINIFRED. Bonnie, what about your father—?

MAXINE. *I'll* look after him, Mrs. Flinder— (*Starts for stairs.*) Good night, Waldo. I had a simply marvelous time! (*Exits up, during:*)

BONNIE. I'm glad *somebody* did!

GUNTHER. I'll see to Nora. You look after your mother. (*Exits to kitchen.*)

WALDO. (*Hands horseshoe to* WINIFRED.) We'll, if you'll excuse me, I have to go home and put out a saucer of milk—maybe a couple of quarts! (*Exits through patio.*)

WINIFRED. (*Starts for stairs.*) I'd better see if Maxine can manage— (*Sees look on* BONNIE'S *face, stops.*) Is anything the matter, dear?

BONNIE. Is *anything* the *matter*—!?

WINIFRED. I mean besides anything I *know* is the matter, darling. What—?

BONNIE. Mother. Can you—*prove* you spent the past two weeks in Paris?

WINIFRED. I don't follow you, dear . . .

BONNIE. What's to follow!? *Can* you *prove* it?!

WINIFRED. Don't you believe—?

BONNIE. Mother—Philip says he is *not* going to return that money. He says you *were* in the hospital—that you were nowhere *near* Paris!

WINIFRED. But surely, darling, the hospital—

BONNIE. Mother, Philip Morgan *runs* that hospital. He's chairman of the board. He pays everybody's salary— recommends nurses for pay increases and evaluates interns for important medical posts. If he says you were there, *they'll* say you were there. Besides, with hundreds of patients coming and going every week, they can't even be certain you *weren't* there. Can you *prove* you weren't—!?

WINIFRED. Well, of *course* I can pr—! . . . Oh, dear!

BONNIE. That's what I was afraid of. Mother, what have you done?

WINIFRED. I—I was afraid of running into any of our friends . . .

BONNIE. So you didn't go to any of our usual hotels, right?

WINIFRED. (*Nods unhappily.*) And I wore a dark black wig and different makeup, in case I just *might* run into anybody who—well—

BONNIE. Did you say you were an American? Are there any bellboys, or hotel clerks, or waiters—?

WINIFRED. Well, darling—you *know* how they over-charge tourists—and I *do* speak French like a native, so—I—

BONNIE. You went around under an assumed name—posing as a visitor from the provinces?

WINIFRED. Fifi Fond du Lac. I wore bangles and a slit skirt.

BONNIE. How about your passport? You had to have it to get into the country, right?

WINIFRED. I used Hermione Mulligan's. I found it in a drawer of her dresser at that soiree last month, when I was looking for a cleansing tissue. She never goes any-place—you know Michael Mulligan! That's what gave me the idea to go to Paris in the first place.

BONNIE. Have you still got it?

WINIFRED. It was void as of today at noon. That's why I settled for two weeks instead of a month. As soon as I cleared customs, I threw it away. Of course, there's the negligee and the perfume—

BONNIE. Which you could get right in Manhatten at any good shop.

WINIFRED. Oh, dear! Does this mean Philip gets to keep the money?

BONNIE. I—I don't know, Mother . . .

WINIFRED. Bonnie, you do *believe* my story—don't you—? (*When* BONNIE *does not reply:*) Oh— Oh, Bonnie! (*Flees upstairs in tears, carrying horseshoe.* BONNIE *stands staring after her, then sits resolutely down on sofa, staring miserably straight out front; after a moment,* GUNTHER *enters from kitchen.*)

GUNTHER. Nora's gone to bed to await the murderer. Is there anything I can do for you before I go, Miss Flinder . . . ?

BONNIE. Just close the patio doors as you go out, huh?

GUNTHER. Oh, sure. (*Starts doing so; then, just before he steps outside:*)

BONNIE. (*Half-turns head.*) Oh, yes, just one more thing, Gunther—

GUNTHER. Yes—?

BONNIE. On your way home, if you should happen to come upon a tiny little creature seated on a mushroom— (*Faces down front for:*) —*step* on him! (*As* BONNIE *glumly props her chin on her fists,* GUNTHER *stands where he is, staring in bemusement at her, as:*)

THE CURTAIN FALLS

ACT THREE

*Curtain-rise finds the stage apparently empty, though
we can hear a faint, hollow HAMMERING noise
from Upstage Left, proceeding in fits and starts—a
tap, silence, a series of rapid bangs, silence, a few
clunks, etc. Outside the closed patio doors looms a
chilly gray morning such as sometimes comes to the
eastern seaboard even in summertime. It is about
nine A.M. A moment after curtain-rise, NORA enters
from kitchen. She is in a long nightgown, slippers
and a comfortable bathrobe. Despite these garments,
she also wears her best and dressiest black hat. She
crosses to the fireplace, crouches, and peers into the
large space behind the short pile of stacked cord-
wood on the andirons.*

NORA. Hey, in there! Not so loud! You'll wake up the
whole house! (*HAMMERING stops, and a moment later*
GUNTHER *pokes his head out over logs.*)

GUNTHER. Do you want that flue opened or don't
you!?

NORA. I'm beginning to think I don't. Like as not,
you'll set the house on fire!

GUNTHER. Not much chance of that. I *told* you this
entire fireplace was built by the little people, chimney
and all. We'll never get a fire started till the household
treats them right.

NORA. (*Throws up her hands and straightens, mas-
saging small of her back.*) You're as bad as that lunatic
Doctor Lennimer! Little people, indeed!

GUNTHER. When you've lived in Tarrytown as long as
I have—

NORA. (*Starts for kitchen.*) I know, I know! I'll be just
as crazy as everybody else around here!

76

GUNTHER. Do you deny events have been a bit strange since you moved in?

NORA. (*Turns, arms akimbo.*) You're blaming all the craziness on the little people? No credit at all to any of the larger numbskulls?

GUNTHER. Ah, but what's been *numbing* those larger skulls?! . . . One small saucer of milk outside the back door—that's all it takes, and the strangeness will pass away like a misty dream.

NORA. If I don't pass away first! I'll have none of your heathen practices, thank you!

GUNTHER. If it was whisky for the leprechauns, you'd have it outside the door in a minute!

NORA. (*Pulls her robe tighter about her.*) Don't be talking about things beyond your understanding. Any creature that would do a good deed for a saucer of milk isn't worth the inconvenience to the cow! A whisky-drinking creature is something to reckon with!

GUNTHER. Well, it's bound to keep him in good spirits!

NORA. (*Turns away and marches toward kitchen, but stops without turning at door, and:*) Would you like a cup of coffee while you're working?

GUNTHER. Just leave it outside the back door. (*He pops back inside fireplace; she rolls her eyes heavenward and exits to kitchen; sporadic HAMMERING begins again; after a moment, BONNIE descends stairs, garbed much like NORA, but minus the hat; she starts to cross to sofas, then pauses, listening to the hammering, and finally looks toward the fireplace; seeing no one, she hesitantly approaches it and leans over to look inside.*)

BONNIE. Is—is somebody there? (*HAMMERING stops.*) Who is it? What are you doing in there?

GUNTHER. (*Pokes head out.*) Would you believe nailing up another horseshoe?

BONNIE. In this house, I'd believe anything! . . . Gunther—what *are* you up to?

GUNTHER. Mrs. Larkin thought a cozy fire would take the chill off the morning.

BONNIE. Do you always light the logs from the far side? *That* ought to unchill you in a hurry!

GUNTHER. Something's jamming the flue. It feels like something up above is holding it shut.

BONNIE. (*Straightens.*) Probably thousands of bats. Does this place have a belfry? No, don't tell me till I've had my morning coffee. *Nora—?!*

NORA. (*Enters with mug of coffee.*) Good morning, dear. Isn't it a dreary day! I thought a fire would be nice.

BONNIE. It was probably a day like this that gave Nero his start! (*Takes coffee.*) Is this for me?

GUNTHER. No.

BONNIE. (*Takes a sip.*) Mmm, that's delicious!

GUNTHER. Oh, good. Now *I* won't have to find out for myself!

BONNIE. You have the fireplace to keep you warm.

NORA. I'll get you another cup, Mister Chowdy. (*Starts for kitchen.*)

BONNIE. Nora— (NORA *turns.*) I love your hat.

NORA. It's the best one I own. I wouldn't want to leave it behind. (*Exits to kitchen.*)

BONNIE. (*Turns toward* GUNTHER.) Say, *are* we expecting a fire?

GUNTHER. Nora told me one more crazy event and she's leaving this place, without stopping for anything. She just believes in being prepared. (*He pops back inside fireplace, and* BONNIE *sits on sofa;* WINIFRED, *also in nightgown, slippers and robe, descends stairs into room.*)

WINIFRED. Did we have hors d'oeuvres last night?

BONNIE. No, we didn't.

WINIFRED. (*Comes to sit beside* BONNIE.) That's a relief. Good morning, dear.

BONNIE. Good morning, Mother. Why is it a relief?

WINIFRED. I couldn't remember having any. I thought it was creeping senility. (*Sporadic HAMMERING begins again.*) *I* don't hear strange noises coming from the fireplace. Do I?

BONNIE. Senility creeps again! That's Gunther. His parents gave him a hammer for his birthday.

WINIFRED. That's nice. Would I be an old silly if I asked what he's trying to accomplish in there?

BONNIE. Nora wants a fire, and no one could think of a good objection. (*HAMMERING stops.*)

WINIFRED. Is he fixing the flue?

GUNTHER. (*Leans out of fireplace.*) No. it refuses to be fixed. I'm simply making a gallant effort. (*As* NORA *enters with another mug of coffee.*) Nora, I don't suppose you have a sledgehammer?

NORA. No, this is a cup of coffee.

WINIFRED. Why, thank you, Nora. How thoughtful. (*Takes mug.*)

GUNTHER. Be my guest. (*Pops back inside fireplace.*)

NORA. I'll try again, Mister Chowdy. (*Turns toward kitchen.*)

WINIFRED. Nora, why didn't we have hors d'oeuvres last night? I distinctly remember discussing them with you.

NORA. Do you distinctly remember I also had to get out the ice bucket, and put up with a stream of traffic in my kitchen? Every time I reached for the potato chips, somebody else barged in.

WINIFRED. I only remember Tony going in there, when Addison and I wanted to be alone and talk.

BONNIE. Well, that explains it: You can't create canapes when you're vying with the company for ear space at a closed door.

NORA. Miss Bonnie, you should be ashamed of yourself for suggesting such a thing! (*Starts out, pauses for:*) And if I were you, Mrs. Flinder, I'd think twice before joining the convent! . . . I've seen the new habits. (*Exits.*)

WINIFRED. There it is again! Why do people keep talking about convents?!

BONNIE. You can only say so much about the weather. (*HAMMERING starts.*)

WINIFRED. You don't understand. That's what your father got so mad about.

BONNIE. The weather?

WINIFRED. No, about my joining the convent. He was quite concerned.

BONNIE. I can't imagine why. It's nowhere near as expensive as a trip to Paris.

WINIFRED. He doesn't know about that. He thinks I made it up. (*Sets mug on table, sighs.*) *Everybody* thinks I made it up . . .

BONNIE. (*Sets her own mug on table.*) I don't.

WINIFRED. When I went upstairs to bed last night— you said—

BONNIE. I'm sorry for what I said. Really, terribly sorry, Mother. (*HAMMERING stops.*) I'd had a rough evening. I simply wasn't thinking straight. But afterwards, sitting down here, alone, I knew it had to be true.

WINIFRED. What convinced you?

BONNIE. It was exactly the crazy kind of thing you'd do to try and help Dad. It was shortsighted, farfetched, and extremely stupid. So I knew you had to be perfectly normal.

GUNTHER. (*Clambering out of fireplace.*) Have you ever thought of buying an electric space heater?

BONNIE. The brownies would just create a power failure.

GUNTHER. Then you know about the fireplace!

BONNIE. Maxine came back downstairs last night for a glass of hot milk. Waldo had told her about it, and she told me.

WINIFRED. I wish someone would tell *me!*

GUNTHER. The fireplace is supposed to be built by brownies. They hate houses without them. They like to huddle there on winter nights.

BONNIE. When the frost is on the mushroom. I don't blame them.

WINIFRED. Surely you two don't *believe* that?

BONNIE. I'll be honest—I don't know. There's certainly

something about this place that—well— Things have a
way of going *wrong* . . .

WINIFRED. It certainly would explain the Carmelites!

GUNTHER. Oh, that reminds me— (*Takes pamphlet
from pocket.*) This must be yours. I accidentally walked
off with it last night.

WINIFRED. (*Takes it, looks, reacts.*) Good heavens!
No wonder your father was upset! I thought we were
talking about yoga lessons!

BONNIE. I might have known we could eventually place
the blame on Lorelei Gullock. Ever since she telephoned
yesterday morning, this place has been a disaster area!

WINIFRED. Now, don't be harsh, Bonnie. I'm sure
Lorelei *meant* to give me the right pamphlet. At least it
wasn't a brochure on diamond-smuggling! (NORA *enters
with third mug of coffee.*)

GUNTHER. (*Grabs mug.*) *Bingo!*

NORA. Three times is the charm. (*Exits to kitchen.*)

WINIFRED. Tell me—both of you—honestly— Is Nora
wearing a hat?

BONNIE. What would you do if I said no?

WINIFRED. Say it and see!

BONNIE. Nora isn't wearing a hat.

WINIFRED. (*Hamming it up lightly:*) Then it's happened! All is lost! I'm going mad—mad—mad—!

ADDISON. (*Off; from staircase vicinity.*) Oh, no!

WINIFRED. (*Grimacing with dismay.*) Oh, no!

BONNIE. Oh, yes!

GUNTHER. The brownies strike again!

ADDISON. (*Enters in pajamas, robe, slippers and a
bulky gauze-and-tape bandage over one eyebrow.*) Winifred—my darling—is there anything I can do?

WINIFRED. Pretend you didn't hear what I said.

ADDISON. I only wish I could. Oh, my dearest darling—!

BONNIE. (*Takes her mug, rises.*) I think I'll go upstairs
and slip into something uncomfortable.

GUNTHER. Shall I get back in the fireplace?

ADDISON. The *fireplace—?!*

GUNTHER. Repair work.

BONNIE. A case of the flue.

WINIFRED. Bonnie, please!

BONNIE. I'm going, I'm going! (*Exits up stairs, on:*)

GUNTHER. I'll go help Nora keep her ears to herself. (*Exits to kitchen, on:*)

WINIFRED. Bless you, Mister Chowdy! (*To* ADDISON.) Now, darling, come and sit here beside me. We have a bit of straightening-out to do.

ADDISON. (*Sits, apprehensively; then:*) Whatever you have to say, darling, I want you to know that I believe you.

WINIFRED. Oh, that's just great! Addison, I do *not* want to be *humored!* (*Hands him pamphlet.*) Exhibit A: Does this look like a booklet on learning yoga?

ADDISON. (*Stares at it; then:*) Oh, certainly, Winifred. Yes, indeed.

WINIFRED. (*Losing patience.*) Addison, we're not going to get anywhere if you keep on *believing* me this way!

ADDISON. Would you rather I didn't? I'll be glad *not* to . . . !

WINIFRED. (*Stares out front, wide-eyed with a sudden horrible notion.*) You know what I just realized? I've poisoned the well!

ADDISON. I'm sure you meant it for the best.

WINIFRED. Not a *real* well, Addison!

ADDISON. Oh, no, of course not.

WINIFRED. Darling, didn't you ever study logical fallacies in school?

ADDISON. Are you changing the subject?

WINIFRED. Far from it! Don't you remember what "poisoning the well" means? One man calls another man a liar. When the second man says it's not true, the first man says, "Ha! Who believes a liar?!" In other words, once the well is poisoned, the damage is almost irreversible. And that's the spot I'm in, right now.

ADDISON. I don't understand.

WINIFRED. You're operating on the premise that I'm unbalanced. Therefore, everything I say, no matter how logical, you dismiss as simple-minded raving.

ADDISON. (*Too heartily.*) Nonsense! Why, you're perfectly fine. Perfectly fine.

WINIFRED. Oh, darling, don't you see— (*She stops as* MAXINE *trots downstairs, garbed in a beguiling sports outfit—tennis shorts, bright shirt, and very colorful sneakers; her mood is bubbly and irrepressibly ecstatic.*)

MAXINE. Good morning! Good morning! Isn't it a lovely day! Did everybody sleep well?

WINIFRED. I take it you did?

ADDISON. You certainly *look* well rested. What happened to your hysterics?

MAXINE. I got to thinking about what Waldo told me about the brownies, and I decided, well, if you can't beat 'em, join 'em!

WINIFRED. You've become a brownie?

MAXINE. I mean, treat them properly. I put out a glass of warm milk for them last night, and I slept like a baby.

ADDISON. Why *warm* milk?

MAXINE. It's a wonderful nightcap when you can't get to sleep. I figured if *they* went to sleep, they couldn't cause any more trouble, and then *I* could sleep.

WINIFRED. There's a certain crazy logic to that, you know it?!

MAXINE. Waldo's taking me to Sunnyside, today. That's where Washington Irving used to live. He's dead, now.

WINIFRED. Oh, what a shame.

ADDISON. (*With some asperity.*) Miss Threadgill—you were hired to look after my wife, not to use our home as a base of operations!

MAXINE. Oh, I wouldn't think of operating here. It's not sterile.

ADDISON. I am talking about your social life!

MAXINE. Why?

WINIFRED. Addison, let the poor child go. I don't really need a nurse . . .

ADDISON. Any woman in your condition who thinks she doesn't need a nurse needs a nurse! (*To* MAXINE:) Miss Threadgill, why did you even *pack* such an outfit?!

MAXINE. Well—*you* know—you never *know* . . . if you know what I mean.

ADDISON. No.

WINIFRED. Maxine, it's all right. You go ahead and have a nice time.

ADDISON. Are you defying my *orders?!*

WINIFRED. Are you *giving* me orders?! Because if you *are*, dearest heart—! (*The PHONE rings.*)

ADDISON. Oh, damn! Miss Threadgill, would you get that? (*As she moves obediently to phone:*) And don't forget to answer with the name of the firm!

MAXINE. (*Nods, picks up phone, and says brightly:*) Good morning! Bellevue! . . .

ADDISON. (*Bolts to his feet on:*) *My* firm, you butter-brain! (*Lurches toward her.*)

MAXINE. But I—

ADDISON. *Give* me that! (*Takes phone;* MAXINE *dissolves into tears, covers her face and rushes upstairs.*)

WINIFRED. (*Rises.*) Addison, you didn't have to—

ADDISON. *Quiet!* Can't you see I'm on the telephone!?

WINIFRED. Anyone who shouts as loudly as *you* doesn't need a telephone! (*Grabs up coffee mug, exits to kitchen.*)

ADDISON. (*Quivers, then controls himself for:*) Hello? . . . Hank! When did *you* get in town? . . . You have? That's wonderful! . . . Yes, by all means, bring them right over! . . . You have our new address? . . . Right! See you soon! . . . 'Bye! (*As he hangs up,* BONNIE *descends stairs, in skirt, sweater and modish boots.*)

BONNIE. Dad, what did you say to Maxine—?

ADDISON. Not half enough! She hasn't done a lick of work since I hired her!

BONNIE. That bandage didn't just *sprout* on your forehead.

ADDISON. Oh. That. Well, you know what I mean! Here she is, ready to go chasing all over the countryside with Doctor Lennimer, while your poor mother—!

BONNIE. Dad, please—your blood pressure! If you'll just let Mother talk with you—

ADDISON. I did! And do you know what she talked about? Poisoning wells!

BONNIE. Not about the convent?

ADDISON. Now, don't *you* start!

BONNIE. (*Indicates pamphlet on table.*) Have you even *looked* at that pamphlet?

ADDISON. Of course I have! She said she thought it was about yoga! No one in their right mind could make a mistake like that!

BONNIE. Mrs. Gullock did . . . Of course, that doesn't disprove your point. (WALDO *appears outside patio doors and raps.*)

ADDISON. Oh, fine, it's the lovelorn neighbor! That's all we need! (*Starts for stairs.*) You talk to him! I have to get some clothes on. Hank will be here any minute!

BONNIE. Hank? Who's Hank?

ADDISON. (*At foot of stairs.*) Henri Marnier. A market research man. He works for Duval in our Paris office. (*Starts up.*)

BONNIE. (*Has started toward* WALDO, *but suddenly stops, looks back.*) Did you say—our *Paris* office? (*But he has gone, and* WALDO *raps again.*) All right, all right! You can *see* I'm coming—! (*Admits* WALDO, *shuts door again on:*) I don't think Maxine can come out and play, today. She's been a naughty girl.

WALDO. Can I sit in the corner *with* her?

BONNIE. (*Points to stairs.*) Second door on the left when you reach the top. (*As he starts up:*) And behave yourself! She's on twenty-four-hour call!

WALDO. Call loud. We'll have the door closed. (*As he vanishes up stairs, front door CHIMES sound;* BONNIE *exits through foyer to answer door; as she does so,* GUN-THER *enters from kitchen, calling back over his shoulder:*)

GUNTHER. Thanks for the coffee! I'll get back at that flue! (*As he clambers back inside fireplace, we hear:*)

LORELEI. (*Off Left.*) Bonnie, I've got to speak to your mother about Tony! (BONNIE *and* LORELEI *enter from foyer, on:*)

BONNIE. What's the matter, Mrs. Gullock? Is he all right?

LORELEI. He's going to quit school! He says modern psychiatry is for the birds! Bonnie—he's thinking of becoming an *astrologer!*

BONNIE. Well, if it's any help—Mother's a Taurus . . .

WINIFRED. (*Enters from kitchen on:*) Did I hear—? Lorelei! How nice! And how early! (*Picks up pamphlet from table.*) But I'm glad to see you anyhow. There's something I want to show you. (*Off Upstage Left, we hear:*)

MAXINE. (*Screams shrilly:*) Aaaaaaah! Waldo!

BONNIE. They promised to close the door.

WINIFRED. What's Waldo doing up there? Maxine is changing clothes.

BONNIE. *Now* you tell me!

WALDO. (*Gallops swiftly down stairs.*) I'll wait in the living room—! (*Sees trio, stops.*) Oh. I hope I didn't intrude—?

BONNIE. Can't you remember?

LORELEI. Doctor Lennimer, thank heaven you're here!

BONNIE. When he could be back *there?* (*Points upstairs.*)

LORELEI. (*Rushing to* WALDO.) You've got to help me save Tony's career! His entire future is at stake! You're the only one who can do it!

WINIFRED. Tony wants piano lessons?

LORELEI. No! After last night—Tony believes in brownies!

BONNIE. Well, anybody would.

WALDO. Mrs. Gullock, what has that got to do with me?

LORELEI. *You* were the one who kept bringing them *up!*

If you tell him it's all nonsense, he'll listen to you! Tell him it was all a joke! (*HAMMERING starts inside fireplace.*) . . . What was that?

WALDO. Sounds like hammering, inside the fireplace. (*It stops.*)

LORELEI. Isn't that the fireplace the *brownies* built—!?

WINIFRED. I thought you didn't believe in brownies?

LORELEI. I said I didn't want *Tony* believing in them! I can believe anything I want.

WINIFRED. Would you believe this is a pamphlet on yoga? (*Hands it over.*)

LORELEI. (*Squints at it, obviously does not see it clearly enough to understand.*) Finished so soon?

WINIFRED. If you mean my marriage, I think the answer may be yes! Lorelei, that's a recruiting brochure from the Carmelites!

LORELEI. You know, I *thought* that girl was rather overdressed for yoga. (*Pops pamphlet into purse.*) What did you say about your marriage—?

WINIFRED. (*Sees WALDO is all ears.*) Look, I'll tell you when the room's less crowded. Why don't you sit down and try to relax? I'll be dressed in a minute. Then— (*Starts upstairs.*) when we're alone—

LORELEI. That may not be for awhile. Philip is bringing Tony over. I thought seeing things in the light of day might snap him out of his unfortunate attitude.

BONNIE. Who? Philip or Tony?

WINIFRED. (*On stairs.*) We'll split them up. *One* of us may have a successful session! (*Exits up stairs.*)

WALDO. If you're trying to avoid crowds, I'll be glad to take Maxine out for awhile . . .

BONNIE. While you're at it, will you please tell her you're not a *medical* doctor?

WALDO. She *knows* I'm not a medical doctor.

BONNIE. Well, she talks as if you were another Albert Schweitzer!

WALDO. Really? It must have been my piano-playing, huh?

BONNIE. She's heard you play?

WALDO. Well—no—but when she stopped by, yesterday, I *showed* her the piano . . .

BONNIE. Yes, but did you tell her what it *was?!* (*Front door CHIMES sound.*)

LORELEI. That must be Philip, with my poor nephew. When you let him in—try to act as if there's nothing wrong. (*HAMMERING starts again.*) *I* don't hear anything! I'll just wait in the kitchen . . . (*Exits swiftly.*)

WALDO. She forgot her purse. I'll take it to her— (*Starts for kitchen, grabs strap of purse en route, purse remains solidly on floor as he passes, almost yanking him off his feet; he lurches back, can barely heft it with both hands, and staggers out, on:*) Good grief! This thing weighs more than *I* do—! (*CHIMES sound again;* BONNIE *hurries out through foyer; as she vanishes,* ADDISON—*casually dressed, bandage still in place—comes down stairs into room.*)

BONNIE. (*Off.*) Oh! I thought you were somebody else!

HENRI. (*Off.*) My name is Henri Marnier. This *is* the Flinder residence—? (*HAMMERING stops.*)

ADDISON. (*Calls.*) Hank, is that you? Come on in, let me have a look at you! (*As* HENRI *and* BONNIE *enter:*) Say, you're a sight for sore eyes. Bonnie, you remember Hank from our Paris trip last year, don't you?

HENRI. (*Shakes head.*) We did not meet. When you conducted your business, your wife and daughter, you said, were out shopping.

ADDISON. That's right. I'd forgotten. Well, this is my daughter, Bonnie— (*Before* HENRI *can even acknowledge the introduction, continues:*) —and now let's get down to business, shall we? Did you bring the stuff? (*Sits on sofa, beckons* HENRI *to join him there, during:*)

HENRI. (*Holds up attaché case.*) I have it all right here . . . samples of three new fragrances that are going to set the world of men's toiletry into a tailspin! (*Sits beside* ADDISON, *opens lid of case upon table.*) *Voilà!*

Go ahead and sample them. I think you will find my judgment is correct!

BONNIE. May *I* have just a little sniff? I *love* anything that smells of Paris— (*Lifts out small bottle, starts to uncork it.*)

HENRI. *Ma'm'selle,* I do not know if you ought to—

ADDISON. Nonsense, Hank! If I can't trust my own daughter to keep a secret, who the heck *can* I trust—?! (*At this point,* BONNIE *has just taken a sniff, and staggered back a pace, causing him to finish:*) What's the matter, Bonnie?

BONNIE. (*Gasping.*) It— It smells like concentrated *garlic!*

HENRI. *Épatant!* You have the good nose! That is exactly what it is!

ADDISON. (*A bit stunned.*) And the other two . . . ?

HENRI. (*Lifting another small bottle.*) Essence of the caves of *Roquefort,* and— (*Lifting final bottle.*) —attar of *oregano!* When a man is wearing these scents, do you know what he will be?!

BONNIE. (*Hands him recorked bottle.*) A walking pizza!

HENRI. (*Pleased.*) *Exactement!* Or rather, that is correct, but what I was going to say is that a man wearing such scents will be *irresistible!* (*Makes classic French gesture: bunches fingertips and thumb, kisses bunched tip and splays them wide open.*)

BONNIE. Maybe in *Milano—!*

ADDISON. Frankly, Hank, you have me confused—I thought you were bringing me the latest aromatic rages from Paris—

HENRI. (*Rises, raising forefinger dramatically.*) But that is exactly what I *do* bring to you! These—yes, these mouth-watering odors—*are* the as-you-say latest aromatic rages. I have done my marketing research for old Duval, and we have come upon an inescapable fact: What is the one thing that all American women have, the one thing that controls their every waking moment, at any hour of day or night?!

BONNIE. An *appetite?!*

HENRI. (*With an eloquent shrug.*) *Mais certainement!* It must be so, *n'est-ce pas?* What do they advertise upon the television—is it the whipped cream upon the hot fudged sundae? No! It is the girdle! It is the diet cola! It is the low-calory Kellogg's K!

ADDISON. And you think— (*Rises, with growing excitement.*) —you think that a man who smells like a square meal—?

HENRI. He will drive them into drooling madness of desire for him!

ADDISON. Bonnie—you're a girl—

BONNIE. Thanks for noticing.

ADDISON. Tell me, honestly—what do *you* think?

BONNIE. Much as I hate to admit it— I think he's *got* something there! But I'm not absolutely sure about the garlic . . .

HENRI. Ah, but you do not yet understand! Yes, you are right. The garlic, it *is* of too strong a smell. But we do not use this alone, you see? We sell the items as a set, with the garlic scent the mildest strength of all, in the hair spray.

ADDISON. How about the others?

HENRI. The oregano is used to give subtle fragrance to the deodorant, and the cheese aroma is placed in the after-shave and cologne.

BONNIE. I can understand the appetite part, but—what made you pick on the pizza-smells?

HENRI. Our market research showed that Americans— no matter what their ethnic background—have one food that is loved and enjoyed by for all practical purposes everybody. That is pizza, no?

ADDISON. That is pizza, yes! Hank, this is magnificent! We'll scoop the entire competition! This must be top secret! Bonnie, get on the phone and call an emergency meeting of all my top chemists and publicity men. Hurry!

BONNIE. (*Headed for phone.*) Any particular time of day?

ADDISON. No later than two o'clock this afternoon. I want this stuff on the market before the back-to-college ads hit the media, end of this month!

BONNIE. Right! (*Starts dialing phone.*)

HENRI. I am glad you like the new idea.

ADDISON. Like it? I adore it! And I'm not going to forget who told it to me, either. You can expect an extra something in your next pay envelope, my boy! Not just a bonus, but a raise, too! (*Both men sit on sofa again.*)

HENRI. *Magnifique!* It could not happen at a better time! You see, *M'sieu* Flinder—I, Henri Marnier, have at last found love!

ADDISON. That's just great, Hank! Who is she?

HENRI. Her name is Fifi Fond du Lac! (*At phone, back to audience,* BONNIE *freezes, abruptly hangs up, then slowly turns face toward men; her expression is one of stark horror.*)

ADDISON. Bonnie, what is it? You look ghastly!

BONNIE. . . . The line's busy!

ADDISON. Is *that* all?! I thought somebody was dead!

BONNIE. That reminds me, I have to check on Mother—— (*Starts for stairs.*) Be right back!

ADDISON. Bonnie, your mother can wait! I want that meeting arranged! (*Turns to* HENRI:) Say! Do you play golf?

HENRI. Every so often, when I go to Scotland to re- search the heather. It is hard to research in Scotland. Even when they like a smell, they do not buy.

ADDISON. (*Rises.*) Well, listen, I've just had a putting green put in, out back. Come on and have a look at it! You can tell me about Fifi!

HENRI. (*Following him toward patio doors.*) Ah, *ma petite Fifi!* Even at the mention of her name, my heart leaps madly within my breast— (*HAMMERING starts.*) *Sacre bleu!* (*Holds hand on chest, blinks in wonderment, exits to patio behind* ADDISON; BONNIE *instantly springs*

for stairs, only to be blocked by MAXINE—*in uniform
again, but minus the cape—just coming down.*)

MAXINE. (*Stopping on bottom step.*) Where is my
Waldo—? I want to apologize for screaming.

BONNIE. *I'm* going to have to apologize for screaming
if you don't get out of my *way—I* (*HAMMER stops.*)
Stand aside! I've got to talk to my mother!

GUNTHER. (*Leans out over logs.*) Say, would you see
if there's some kind of handle or release up there on the
outside of this thing—? (*Door CHIMES sound.*)

MAXINE. (*Starts down, re-blocking* BONNIE.) Is that
my Waldo? Let him in!

BONNIE. (*Finally steps down and aside.*) *You* do the
honors! I have a life to save!

MAXINE. (*Moves gaily toward foyer.*) Coming! My
dearest darling, I'm coming! (*Exits toward front door.*)

WALDO. (*Steps in from kitchen.*) Maxine! Who are you
talking to?! (BONNIE *exits up stairs.*)

MAXINE. (*About-faces, reacts.*) I thought that was you
at the door. (*Starts toward him.*) My darling, what's
wrong? Are you in pain?

WALDO. I think I hurt myself picking up Lorelei's purse.
(*Door CHIMES sound.*)

GUNTHER. (*Still over logs.*) Would somebody see if
there's a damper handle up above here?

MAXINE. Damper than what? (ADDISON *and* HENRI
enter from patio.)

ADDISON. Mister Chowdy! My entire putting green is
covered with mushrooms!

GUNTHER. I *told* you this was brownie territory.

WALDO. (*Letting* MAXINE *help him to sofa.*) They're
probably massing for an all-out attack.

HENRI. Why is that man in the fireplace? (*Door
CHIMES sound three times.*)

NORA. (*Enters from kichen.*) Isn't anybody going to
get the door? (*Starts for foyer.*)

LORELEI. (*Enters from kitchen.*) That must be Tony

and Doctor Morgan. Addison, when he comes in, whatever you do, act natural!

BONNIE. (*Descends stairs just as* NORA *exits into
foyer.*) Isn't somebody going to get that door?

ADDISON. Bonnie, my putting green is covered with
mushrooms!

BONNIE. What's that got to do with answering the
door?

GUNTHER. Miss Flinder, would *you* see if there's a
damper handle someplace above the mantelpiece?

MAXINE. It's the strangest thing—all at once I have
a taste for pizza . . . !

HENRI. You see! Already she is driveling!

ADDISON. You mean drooling! . . . Bonnie, where's
your mother?

BONNIE. Well—she—um— (PHILIP *and* NORA *enter,
half-dragging a distraught* TONY *between them.*)

TONY. No! Please! I'll be all right! Just let me go
home! I've got to study for exams!

HENRI. Have I come at a bad time?

BONNIE. Yes! Why don't you go to our Manhattan
office, and Dad will join you there later!

ADDISON. Maybe that's a good idea. (*Outside the patio
doors, an escape-rope of knotted sheets drops into view,
unnoticed by anyone as yet.*)

MAXINE. (*To* PHILIP.) Why don't you bring Tony over
here, where he can sit down?

WALDO. What about my sprained arm?

MAXINE. I'll take care of that in a minute.

ADDISON. Bonnie, would you get your mother? I'd like
Hank to meet her before he leaves.

BONNIE. Well—she may be taking a nap . . .

HENRI. At this hour of the day?

ADDISON. My wife—well—you see, Hank—she's a little
—um—eccentric . . .

NORA. (*Sees wriggling sheets.*) Glory be! What's that?!

BONNIE. The laundry! The dryer's broken, and we're
hanging it out!

ADDISON. (*Starting for patio.*) With *knots* in it?! (*Steps out, looks up.*) Winifred! What do you think you're *doing* up there?!

WINIFRED. (*Off.*) Would you believe—the old yoga rope trick—?!

ADDISON. You get right back inside that window before you kill yourself, and come down the stairs like a normal human being!

HENRI. You say—your wife is a *little* eccentric . . . ?

LORELEI. Why, she's very advanced! The rope trick is at least fifteen chapters after the lotus position! (*As* ADDISON *steps in from patio, and sheets are slowly drawn up out of sight:*)

HENRI. There was something about your wife's voice—

BONNIE. No, there wasn't!

GUNTHER. (*Clambers out of fireplace.*) All right, then, *I'll* look for the damper!

TONY. I'm feeling much better, now. Can I go home?

PHILIP. Not until we get this silly brownies notion out of your head!

HENRI. Perhaps I had better go.

ADDISON. Nonsense! Bonnie, you tell your mother to come downstairs at once!

BONNIE. I'll see what I can do. (*Exits up stairs.*)

GUNTHER. (*Examining space above mantel.*) There's not even a push-button here! It must work by magic.

ADDISON. Philip, I've got to talk to you about Winifred.

PHILIP. This is hardly the place to discuss your wife's mind.

NORA. One madhouse is as good as another! (*Exits to kitchen.*)

HENRI. (*Starts putting bottles back into case.*) I think maybe I will return at some more fortunate time. (WINIFRED *descends stairs, still in nightgown, robe and slippers, but she now wears a hat with a face-hiding veil;* BONNIE *descends immediately behind her, during:*)

ADDISON. Winifred, why are you wearing that hat?

WINIFRED. Nora and I are starting a new fashion trend.

ADDISON. But it looks silly!

LORELEI. New fashions always look silly. (NORA *enters from kitchen, dressed as before, now carrying suitcase.*)

NORA. If you'll excuse me, I've got to finish packing! (*Heads for bar, packs bottle of brandy during:*)

WINIFRED. Now see what you've done, Addison! Nora's leaving, after all these years!

ADDISON. What *I've* done—?!

PHILIP. Now, now! Humor her, remember?!

BONNIE. Humoring Mother is what *started* all this trouble, you quack!

HENRI. (*Closes case, picks it up.*) I, too, am all packed to go!

MAXINE. Oh, Waldo, isn't this exciting!? Nora's running off with a Frenchman!

PHILIP. Addison, I think you should make your daughter apologize for that nasty quack—*crack!*

MAXINE. But you *are* nasty, Doctor Morgan. It's men like you who turn me against the entire medical profession!

WALDO. Really!? Do you really feel that way, Maxine?

MAXINE. I'm sorry, Waldo, but I do.

WALDO. All right! I'll give *up* medicine!

MAXINE. But what will you do for a living, darling?

BONNIE. Say, why don't you become a piano teacher?

MAXINE. Oh, *could* you, Waldo?

WALDO. For you, darling, *anything!*

LORELEI. (*Very bewildered.*) But—Doctor Lennimer *is* a—

BONNIE. (*Interrupts swiftly, sings:*) "—jolly good fellow! Yes—" (WINIFRED *and* GUNTHER *join her for:*)

TRIO. "—he's a jolly good fellow! Oh, he's a jolly good fel-looooow—!"

ADDISON. Have you all gone crazy?!

WALDO. It's the brownies!

TONY. (*Rises.*) Let me out of here!

NORA. (*Taking suitcase onto patio.*) You'll have to get in line!

ADDISON. Nora Larkin, you come back here this minute!

NORA. (*On patio.*) If I did, *I'd* be crazy! (*Steps out of sight.*)

BONNIE. Philip, if you don't tell Dad the truth, I will!

ADDISON. What are you talking about?

BONNIE. Mother never *did* have an operation. She *did* spend the last two weeks in Paris!

PHILIP. This is worse than I feared, Addison. Winifred's condition must be hereditary!

BONNIE. Are you trying to tell Dad that *I'm* nuts, *too?*

WINIFRED. What do you mean, *too?*

BONNIE. You know what I mean! Philip's piling one lie onto another!

ADDISON. Will somebody kindly tell me what is going on here?!

WINIFRED. All right! Addison, I can *prove* that I was in Paris. Henri— (*Takes off hat and veil.*) Tell my husband who I am!

HENRI. *M'sieu* Flinder—this is your wife!

ADDISON. I *know* that!

WINIFRED. Henri—don't you remember your little Fifi Fond du Lac?!

HENRI. Ah, my Fifi! I shall never forget her! That curly black hair—the charming slit skirts—the tinkling bangles—!

BONNIE. *M'sieu Marnier*—you don't understand— Mother *is* your Fifi!

ADDISON. Hank, is this true?

HENRI. Even if it were, a French gentleman would never betray a woman to her husband!

BONNIE. Oh, great! Chivalry's alive again, and we're dead!

NORA. (*Reappears from patio, minus suitcase.*) One more thing, Mr. Flinder—I forget to tell you where to send my final paycheck—

ADDISON. Payday isn't till the fifteenth of the month!

NORA. The least you could do is pro-rate it to the thirteenth!

WINIFRED. Today's the *thirteenth?* It *can't* be the thirteenth!

BONNIE. Mother, what's the matter? Of *course* it's the thirteenth!

WINIFRED. (*Counting on her fingers as she talks.*) But if that's true—let me see—there was the week before Hermione's party—and— (*Sinks slowly to sit on sofa.*) Oh, dear me . . . !

PHILIP. Winifred, what's the matter? You look ghastly!

WINIFRED. I'll tell you what's the matter, you quack! I'm going to have a baby!

BONNIE. (*Drops to knees beside her.*) A baby! You mean, after all these years, I'm going to be a *sister?!*

LORELEI. Now we're back to the *convent* again!

TONY. But—if she's going to have a baby—she couldn't have had that operation!

ADDISON. Hey, that's right! Philip, what is the meaning of this?!

PHILIP. It's a trick! She's lying! I refuse to stay here and be insulted!

BONNIE. You can leave with our blessing, as soon as you give back that check—for services never rendered!

ADDISON. No. Let him keep the check. But when Winifred *does* have the baby, in— How long—?

WINIFRED. About seven months.

ADDISON. Yes, seven months. When she *does* have it. Philip, you can return to me *double* the amount of that check for every single month in the interim.

PHILIP. But that check is for $2500, Addison. In seven months, that would cost me—um—

TONY. Three-hundred-twenty-thousand dollars!

LORELEI. Tony, that's marvelous! Your mind is perfectly fine, if you can do that kind of calculation in your head!

TONY. Aunt Lorelei—you're right! I'm cured!

ADDISON. Philip—are you willing to stake that much money that Winifred is telling a lie?

PHILIP. (*Glumly hands over check to* ADDISON.) Well, of course, I could have been *mistaken* about the operation—

ADDISON. You charlatan! Get out of my house!

NORA. Well, if nobody is really crazy, I'd better get my suitcase— (*Exits through patio.*)

PHILIP. But Addison, this whole plan was your wife's idea, so you could move to the country and get a rest!

ADDISON. You call this a *rest?!*

NORA. (*Off.*) Aaaaaah! It's the brownies! (*She rushes back into room, clutching unlocked suitcase in both arms.*) They took that whole bottle of brandy! (*At Upstage Left, the logs in fireplace begin to flicker and glow.*)

MAXINE. Waldo, take me out of here!

WALDO. (*Rises, starts escorting her toward patio.*) But Maxine—the brownies are going to be *friendly,* now—!

LORELEI. *Now,* but did you ever have a brandy hangover?!

TONY. I want to go home!

LORELEI. Come on, Tony. (*Leads him toward foyer.*) I have some splendid books on astrology you can borrow. (*As they exit through foyer:*)

BONNIE. What'll you bet he winds up in the convent!?

MAXINE. (*As she and* WALDO *exit through patio:*) Waldo, darling, where are you taking me?

WALDO. To my place, of course. *You're* going to see me *operate!* (MAXINE *giggles in anticipation as they exit, arm in arm.*)

GUNTHER. Hey, the fire started by itself!

BONNIE. Well, that brandy *is* forty-eight dollars a bottle.

HENRI. (*To* WINIFRED.) *Madame* . . . if it should be a baby girl—

WINIFRED. If you think I'm going to call her Fifi, you must think I *am* crazy!

ADDISON. Say—if Winifred's story is true—*did* you know her in Paris?!

HENRI. Did I mention Fifi's birthmark to you?

ADDISON. No, you didn't—?

HENRI. Good! Then your wife and I did *not* meet in Paris! (BONNIE *and* WINIFRED *cover their eyes.*) Besides, Fifi's birthmark was on the *left* side!

ADDISON. How did you know Winifred's was on the *right?!*

GUNTHER. (*Heads for bar.*) I think I'd better put a few more bottles outside. The brownies have a lot of work in store for them!

BONNIE. (*Starts for bar.*) You'd better leave a little for me and Mother—!

PHILIP. Maybe I'd better stick around—I have the feeling someone is going to need a doctor—!

WINIFRED. Addison, I can explain—!

ADDISON. Winifred, what is this man to you—?

HENRI. Let us discuss this matter like gentlemen—!

NORA. My, but it's getting *warm* in here—!

VOICE. (*Deep, disembodied and booming.*) First, say goodbye to all the nice people—then hurry up with that brandy!

ALL. (*Have reacted to* VOICE; *then turn heads right out front, and speak directly to audience:*) Goodbye, nice people! (*CURTAIN starts down, during:*)

ADDISON. Winifred, about this baby—

HENRI. I assure you, *M'sieu* Flinder, my relationship with Fifi was—

WINIFRED. Addison, don't you remember, the night before Hermione's party when you and I—

BONNIE. Gunther, would you care to join me in a brandy—?

NORA. *I* certainly would—!

ADDISON. I intend to get to the bottom of this—!

WINIFRED. Addison, darling, your blood pressure—! (*Fireplace flames burn brightly, as all onstage turn to point a finger at another person, as follows:* ADDISON *to*

HENRI, HENRI *to* WINIFRED, WINIFRED *to* PHILIP, PHILIP *to* ADDISON, BONNIE *to* NORA, NORA *to* GUNTHER, *and* GUNTHER *to* BONNIE.)

ALL. (*Simultaneously, with pointing finger:*) Now listen, just a minute—! (*All turn and point to person who was just pointing at them, on:*) And *you* keep out of it—!

(*THE CURTAIN IS DOWN.*)

PROPERTIES

ACT ONE

PRESET:

Plenty of liquor in bottles behind bar, with a wide assortment of glasses (snifter, highball, etc.)

Carried on by:

BONNIE:

Armful of gladiolas, wristwatch on wrist

NORA:

Bowl for gladiolas, small pitcher of water, bottle of aspirin, sandwich on plate

ADDISON:

Small overnight bag

MAXINE:

Wristwatch

LORELEI:

Huge purse, stocked with stack of rubber-banded pamphlets, pair of sneakers, garish novel, box of chocolates, small crowbar, teddy bear

WALDO:

Two gladiolas

GUNTHER:

Cap, horseshoe, empty plate

ACT TWO

PRESET:

Glasses and large pitcher for Manhattans at bar, bowl of gladiolas on table, pamphlet on table

Carried on by:

NORA:

Ice bucket filled with cubes for Manhattans

PHILIP:

Check in pocket

LORELEI:

Huge purse with huge flashlight inside it

TONY:

Horseshoe

ACT THREE

PRESET:

Knotted sheets ready above patio door, fireplace logs (fake electric) connected to rheostat so "flames" can slowly brighten

Carried on by:

PHILIP:

Check in pocket

GUNTHER:

Pamphlet in pocket

NORA:

Hat, three mugs of coffee (one at a time), large suitcase

ADDISON:

Bandage on forehead

LORELEI:

Purse (twice: into living room, then back into room after WALDO brings off)

HENRI:

Attache case containing three bottles of liquid: clear (garlic), milky (Roquefort), and green (oregano)

WINIFRED:

Hat with veil

SOUND EFFECTS

Two-tone chimes, loud hammering for horseshoe, hollow hammering for flue, metallic clunk, metallic clang, telephone bell, deep hollow voice

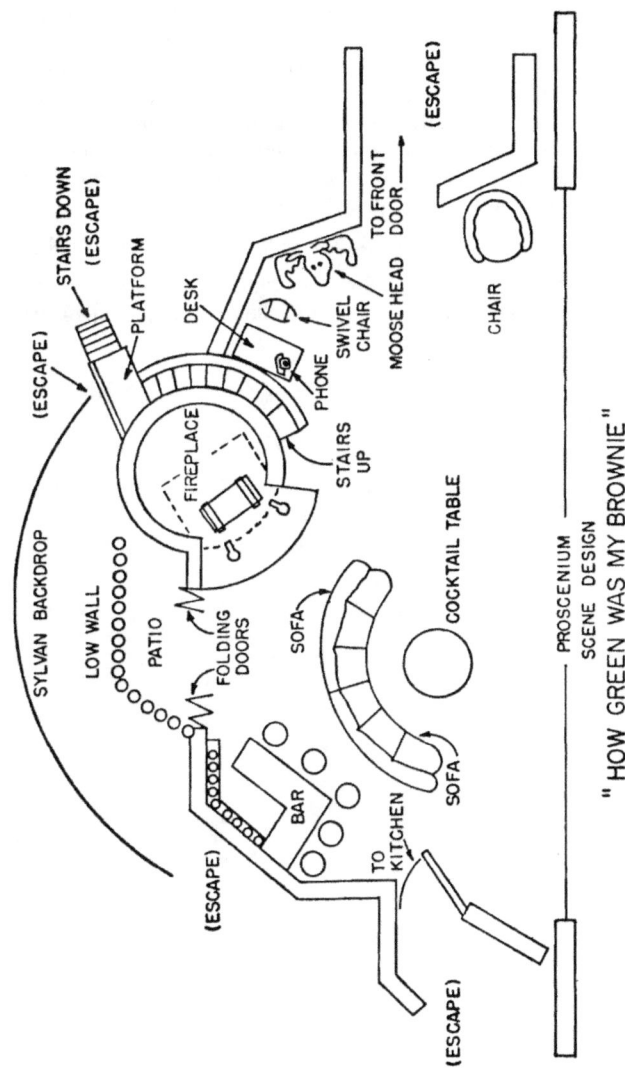

"HOW GREEN WAS MY BROWNIE"

SCENE DESIGN

MUSIC USE NOTE